Patrick Frost is an Australian writer living in Mildura, Victoria.
A *Sky Populated by Tongues* is his first collection.

A SKY
POPULATED
BY
TONGUES

Patrick Frost

Published by Patrick Frost

First published 2021
© 2021 Patrick Frost

The moral right of the author has been asserted.

 A catalogue record for this book is available from the National Library of Australia

ISBN 978 0 6453335 0 3 (pbk)
ISBN 978 0 6453335 1 0 (ebk)

Edited by Mark Macleod
Designed and typeset by Blue Wren Books
Printed by Ingram Spark

Contents

A Sky Populated by Tongues

It is true that the older you get, the more precious your memories become. People come and go, material possessions come and go, but memories stay with you a lifetime. I would like to share with you, if I may, on the eve of my centenary, my most precious memory. This memory has kept me company when I have been at my lowest ebb, it has kept me company when I have stood at the summit of the mountain. It has kept me company when I have been at sea level. At all times it has made itself available to me as a source of inspiration.

On my tenth birthday, almost ninety years ago to the day, I was treated to the most marvellous birthday party a boy could imagine. At the commencement of the party, a cake large enough to feed myself, my parents and the guests was served. After we polished off this delicious treat, the guests formed a circle around me and presented me with the finest gifts a boy could hope to receive, among them a shiny red toy car, a kite that appeared to be itching to take off and a multicoloured yo-yo. At the conclusion of this ritual,

I took a seat and was entertained by the greatest selection of performers ever assembled.

Firstly, a dozen daring acrobats swung from one side of the hall to the other, with no safety net to catch them. Then a brilliant juggler kept an ever-increasing number of objects in the air: bowling balls, then ten pins, plates, cutlery and finally lighted candles! After that, a magician performed every trick in his repertoire, from making a hare appear under a man's hat (Lord Butterworth was an enthusiastic volunteer for this trick) to blowing bubbles, with me ending up in the biggest bubble of all, which popped – coating me entirely in bubble-gum.

When he had finished I went outside and frolicked around the grounds, skipped over rocks and had an all-round grand time. Eventually, however, I began to tire. All the excitement of the day had plain worn me out. Before I knew it, I was leaning against my favourite oak tree, struggling to keep my head upright.

When I woke I sensed that my little finger was encased in wetness. Curious, I looked down and discovered it was being suckled by a goat. It took me some time to realise that it was my bubble-gum coating that had drawn the animal to me. Unafraid, I watched until a sheep ambled up and took my glance away. I don't know how long our eyes were locked together before the animal broke its gaze and began to lick my sleeve with its hardy tongue. As I looked from tongue to tongue, there was a tickling sensation behind my left ear. Without even having to turn around I knew it was my cat Edward.

Even if I had wanted to confirm it, I could not, as my golden retriever George had bounded up to me, set his paws on my chest and started to lick my lips. I looked down and watched his tongue dance about like a ballerina. The sight was so mesmerising that I did not realise my beloved pony Albert had arrived until he pushed his muzzle in between George and the sheep and began to lick my nose; nor a small bird, until I felt its minute tongue dab at the top of my left ear.

As I looked into a sky populated by tongues, a camel made its way into my line of sight. To my surprise it unleashed its mighty tongue onto my lower right leg and busied itself. It was followed in quick succession by a llama, which sloppily attacked my other leg, a zebra which began to suckle my right earlobe, a giraffe which unravelled its sodden appendage onto my forehead and an African elephant which wrapped its soft pink tongue around my torso. What could be next?

A minuscule rodent of some description appeared on the top of Albert's head. I gazed into the creature's crinkly eyes. What did it have in store for me? I did not have to wait too long to find out. The feeble creature parted its lips and sent a diminutive pink tongue slowly toward me.

Floyd

It was six twenty-three when James bounced out of bed. He had endured a long week of school and was ready to devour the weekend as if it were a slice of delicious chocolate cake. After stepping over his toy rocket ship, he opened his bedroom door and began to prance down the hallway. He was headed for the kitchen to fix himself a bowl of cereal.

The hallway ahead of him looked almost like a tunnel. James heard a faint creak. He tensed up and dug his toes into the plush burgundy carpet. Was it Mother? It couldn't be. She got up at exactly seven o'clock. James continued down the hallway past the three portraits his mother had commissioned: the one with him wearing the old-fashioned suit, the one with him in the unicorn costume and the one with him wearing angel wings. He did not want to be caught up and about at this time. The last time that happened Mother wept for hours. He stopped at the three-quarter mark and listened again. Silence. Not a sound. James kept going and turned right into the kitchen.

As he set foot on the cold white tile, a shiver went down his spine. A man he had never seen before was sitting at the kitchen table. James felt he had stepped onto a sprawling tundra he was doomed to inhabit for eternity. This feeling persisted until he stepped back onto the relative safety of the burgundy carpet through sheer force of will and wheeled around the corner out of view.

Despite experiencing abject terror in that moment, James had managed to notice several details. The first was that the man was facing away from the kitchen window. From this, he deduced that the man had not seen him, unless it was out of the corner of his eye, nor heard him, as he had made very little noise due to his being barefoot. James also noticed that the kitchen blind had been raised, allowing the first light of the day to enter the kitchen, illuminating the man and giving him the appearance of a deity. Who was this man? Why was he sitting at the kitchen table? Did he pose a risk to himself and Mother? These questions James had no way of answering.

With his heart thumping in his chest, he craned his neck around the kitchen doorway in order to get another look at the stranger. The man had a sharp nose and blond hair. He was also dressed in a bottle-green suit.

James jerked his head back and ran to his mother's bedroom. With a shaking hand, he turned the doorknob and pushed the door open as quietly as he could so as not to startle her. Before his eyes adjusted to the darkness, the smell of potpourri reached his nostrils.

He could just make out the four-poster bed containing the fragile creature that was his mother. For a split second he considered leaving her be, but ultimately decided his mother needed to be told that their household had been infiltrated.

Approaching his mother's bedside, James observed her, resplendent in her ivory silken nightgown. Her breathing was shallow, almost imperceptible. "Mother?" he said softly. No response. "Mother?" Slightly louder. Still nothing. He placed his hand on her forehead. She woke with a start and stared at her son in horror.

"What's wrong, James?" she said, trembling. "Is there a fire?"

"No," he said. "There's a man in the kitchen. He's been there since I woke up."

"What time is it?" Mother sat up and glanced at her alarm clock. "Six thirty-one!" Tears formed in her eyes.

"You know you're not supposed to get up before seven!" James became upset at the sight of his mother crying and burst into tears himself. Mother and son huddled together and wept.

"What are you going to do about the man in the kitchen?" James said when they had finished.

His mother looked defeated. "What can I do?" she whispered.

The two of them made their way down the hallway silently as ghosts, with Mother in front to shield her son from a possible attack. When she reached the entrance of the kitchen she peered around the corner at the intruder. She jerked her head back as James had moments earlier.

"Have you seen him before?" James asked.

She shook her head.

Mother and son spent the rest of the morning in the parlour. Intermittently, Mother would arm herself with the fireplace poker and pay a visit to the kitchen doorway in order to check on the stranger. Each time she returned with the news that he was still seated at the kitchen table.

"I'm hungry, Mother," James said as the morning melted into the afternoon.

"Hush," she hissed.

In mid-afternoon the sound of the refrigerator door closing reached the parlour. Mother tensed up. "Please refrain from following me, James," she said. She reached the entrance to the kitchen and peered around the corner. Nothing had changed – apart from the glass of orange juice on the table.

"Is he still there?" James mouthed the words at her when she returned.

She nodded.

"And what if he never leaves?"

She stared at nothing in particular. "That is a prospect we may have to get our heads around, sooner rather than later."

James curled up in one of the armchairs and tried to get to sleep, but each time he nodded off he was jolted awake by the rumbling of his stomach.

As afternoon turned to evening, Mother again armed herself with the poker and made her way to the kitchen.

Same as before – except that the glass was now empty. She crept back to the parlour and laid the poker to rest.

"He's sitting in the same place," she said when she noticed James was awake.

He looked at her with a pained expression. "Can't we sneak some food out?" He might have been on the verge of collapse.

She placed her hand on his forehead. "We just can't take that risk."

Before long they found themselves sitting in the dark. After much deliberation, Mother decided it would be best if her and James retired to her bedroom. But first she would check on the intruder one last time. She grabbed the poker and headed back to the kitchen. Once again, almost unchanged – except that the blind had been drawn.

When Mother had tucked James into her bed, she floated over and locked the bedroom door. Upon hearing the reassuring click, she fell to the floor and leant against the door, still with poker in hand. She planned to keep watch throughout the night in case the lock should fail. Several minutes later, however, she fell victim to sleep.

At one point a strange sound jolted her awake. She looked over to her bed. James was fast asleep. The stranger? Despite her briefly heightened senses, she slept.

When dawn broke, James opened his eyes and recognised

nothing. The smell of potpourri maybe. Then flashes of a predicament he and his mother had found themselves in. There she was, propped against the bedroom door, fast asleep. Although weak, he disentangled his legs from her silk sheets and stepped onto the carpet. He collapsed with a thump that woke her.

"James?" she croaked.

That was her son sprawled on the floor. She gasped and lurched forward. "James, don't! Don't leave me alone!" Scooping him up onto her back, she wrenched the door open and stumbled into the hallway.

The stranger would still be at the kitchen table. There was only one thing to do. She summoned all her strength, staggered back down the hallway, turned into the front room and out through the front door into the morning air.

At last, they were all free.

The Waitress

"Lime?"

PJ nodded and watched with an indifferent eye as the waitress set his milkshake down in front of him.

"Blue heaven?"

Lewis swung around on his chair, offered his thanks and reached for the milkshake to save her the trouble of stretching.

"And banana?"

Finch shot the waitress a wink and allowed her to place the milkshake before him. When she was out of earshot Finch leant in to his two friends. "You won't believe what you're about to hear, boys." He leant in closer still. "By the end of the week, I think my parsnips will be ready for harvesting."

PJ suddenly came to life and slapped the counter. "You don't say!"

"It's true!" Finch said as he bounced on his stool.

"With the yams not too far behind." Lewis whistled.

A Pretty Garden

Mr Monroe brushed off his white suit and checked that his waxed moustache was in order as the elderly women arrived. He had put a lot of work into organising today and wanted everything to be perfect, right down to his appearance. "Good morning, ladies!" He wondered whether he was almost shouting, but there were bound to be many in the group who were hard of hearing.

"I'm well, thank you," said one of them named Phyllis.

"I hope each and every one of you will enjoy exploring the garden today," Mr Monroe said. "Make your way at your leisure down these sweeping lawns. Marvel at the annuals. Be dazzled by the perennials! Listen to the birdsong as it floats down from the trees. But most important of all —" At this point he gathered the women into one tight group to make sure his advice was heard. "When you come to the garden bed that is populated almost entirely by radiant yellow flowers, do not – I repeat, do not – take in the scent of the sole purple specimen. I cannot tell you why —" His face was carved from granite. "All I can tell you is that I strictly forbid it." As a beam of sunlight emerged from behind a cloud the smile returned to Mr Monroe's face. "Now that that's out of the way, off you go! Explore!"

"It's so nice of that man to invite us all to come and see his garden," Phyllis said to her friends Shirley and Ruth, as they strolled ahead of the main group. "And to specifically invite ladies who have no family. It just goes to show that there are still kind-hearted people in this world."

"So true," said Shirley. "It really restores your faith in human nature."

"Goodness!" Ruth stopped dead. "Is that a lilli pilli?"

Phyllis and Shirley looked where she was pointing.

"I believe it is." Shirley nodded.

The three of them continued down one of Mr Monroe's sweeping lawns.

"Ah, the good old bottlebrush," Shirley said, gesturing to their right.

"No, thank you," said Phyllis.

"When I was a little girl, my street was lined with these," Ruth said.

"I think everybody's street was," said Shirley. "But there aren't as many around these days." She stopped, deep in thought. "Or maybe there are, and I don't notice them as much as I did then." Her friends had kept walking, so she paced it up in order to catch them.

Mr Monroe was relaxing on his patio with a glass of ginger ale when he spotted a woman walking with some difficulty toward him. He narrowed his eyes. "Good morning!" he chirped when she reached him at last. "Not a fan of the garden?"

She blushed deeply. "Oh, no." She steadied herself on the walking frame. "I think it's lovely. I just need to sit down for a while. My legs are tired."

Mr Monroe giggled. "Oh, I don't believe that for a second. You look like you could walk for days!"

"I wish," she sighed.

He made no response, but topped up his glass. He took a long sip through an elaborate curled straw, then leant back in his wicker chair and suddenly focused on the woman as if he had noticed her for the first time. "Go on, get going," he said cheerfully. "See if you can catch up to the others. And remember what I said – do not sniff that purple flower."

The conversation had come to an end. With great effort, the woman turned her walking frame around and began to trudge after the main group.

Elsewhere in the garden, Pearl came to a fork in the road. "Left or right?" she mumbled to herself. While the left-hand path appeared to lead to a smaller garden, it was difficult to discern where the right-hand path led, as the view was obscured by a large oak tree. "Ain't nobody here to tell me which way to go," she said to herself, and that was true. One of the least popular residents of *The Meadows*, Pearl had been left to her own devices by the others and was hence exploring Mr Monroe's garden at her own pace. She decided to head right.

After crunching across a seemingly never-ending carpet of acorns, she came to a gate. She grabbed it and shook it. When it did not open, she hoisted a withered leg over the top, performed a decidedly unladylike pirouette and found herself on the other side. Much to her surprise, a desert landscape lay before her.

"What the hell," she muttered.

Fitter than most, Phyllis, Shirley and Ruth were soon out of sight of the main group. "Just look at those roses!" Shirley exclaimed. The cobblestoned path cut through a garden containing every variety of rose imaginable.

"I know!" Phyllis bent down and took in the scent of one of the many blood-red blooms. A smile formed on her face. "This smells like a real rose. Not like the ones in the shops." She bent down and sniffed it again. "Yes. That's real, all right." She watched as Shirley bent down too.

"Oh, you're right," Shirley said. "Ruth, you have to smell this."

Ruth knelt dutifully and zeroed in on the rose. "Oh, yes. Oh, that's really strong." Eventually, the three women gathered themselves and continued along the path.

As Ruth stepped off the end of the path and joined Phyllis and Shirley on the lush grass, it began to snow. She looked up at the sky. "The weather's turned quickly," she said.

"I'll say," said Shirley. "It didn't look like it was going to snow five minutes ago." As the snow began to fall more heavily, the women shielded their eyes.

"This is ridiculous," said Phyllis.

Ruth huffed. "I can hardly see a thing."

While the three of them battled what was fast becoming a blizzard, the nine women who made up the main group dawdled along in the sunshine surrounded by an array of tropical plants. Now and then, one of them stopped to take a closer look at something that caught their eye, but generally the group moved as one.

"I can't remember the last time I had so much fun," Dorothy said to no one in particular.

As the group crossed the path taken by Phyllis, Shirley and Ruth, an icy wind blew through them and several women shivered and buttoned their cardigans. As soon as they were past it, however, the tropical breeze that had previously wafted in from the west returned. Confusion reigned, and in no time at all the women were unbuttoning the very cardigans they had just done up.

Like three arctic explorers, Phyllis, Shirley and Ruth struggled against the force of the blizzard.

"I can't see where I'm going, can you?" Shirley called out.

"No, her name's not Gertrude," yelled Phyllis. Ruth braced herself and pushed through the storm until she stumbled and fell face-first into the snow.

"Help!" she managed to cry before the snow covered her completely. Shirley turned in the direction of her friend's voice and forced her way through the snow until she came into contact with a solid lump. Taking a deep breath and bracing herself, she hauled her friend back into an upright position.

Linking arms, the two women pushed on in the direction they had been heading prior to Ruth's tumble. Eventually, they reached Phyllis.

"I thought I'd lost you forever!" cried Phyllis. The three of them came to a set of steps with wrought iron handrails. By the time they had reached the bottom, the snowstorm had ceased, and all was calm once more.

They found themselves in a garden crowded with palm trees, toadstools and exotic plants, including one with saucer-shaped orange and blue flowers, a ground cover that moved intermittently and a crimson-coloured plant that made a hissing noise. In the centre of the garden was a garden bed populated entirely by bright yellow flowers save for one gigantic purple specimen.

"That must be the flower that the man told us not to smell," Phyllis said as the three women gazed on it in awe.

"Must be," agreed Ruth. The women inched closer.

"I wonder why he doesn't want us to smell it," said Phyllis.

Shirley frowned. "There must be some reason."

"Yes, but what?" said Phyllis.

"It could be poisonous," chimed in Ruth.

"But you can't get poisoned just by smelling a flower," said Phyllis.

"Not that I've ever heard," said Shirley. The women inched closer still.

"A little sniff wouldn't matter," said Phyllis. "Anyway, how would he know?"

"Come on, you two," Shirley said. "In for a penny, in for a pound."

The three women gathered around the purple flower. As they were about to take in the scent, a sound not unlike the sky ripping apart rang through the air and they were sucked into the flower headfirst.

"Thank goodness, some steps!" Dorothy said to no one in particular. Murmurs of approval sounded throughout the group. Slowly, the nine women made their way down the steps in single file, each clutching at the handrails. There were murmurs of amazement as each got her first look at the exotic garden.

"There's that flower Mr Monroe told us to stay away from," said a woman named Gertrude when she spotted the deep purple petals.

"But what are those things near it?" said her best friend Iris.

"Why don't you have a closer look instead of squinting?" Dorothy grinned. "The wind will change and you'll be stuck like that, you know."

Iris scowled and moved in. "They're handbags," she

announced. "Three handbags. Don't they belong to Phyllis and Shirley and Ruth? They were walking ahead of us."

Dorothy sniffed. "So, where are they?"

Iris scowled again. "How should I know?" She stood up to get some perspective on the purple flower.

"Don't smell it," Dorothy said quickly. "Remember what the man said."

"Don't tell me what to do!" Iris took a breath. She had barely begun to lean in when a sound not unlike the sky ripping apart was heard and she was sucked into the flower headfirst. The sound got louder. And louder again, as they were sucked into the flower one by one.

It was mid-afternoon by the time Myrtle reached the steps. Despite her best efforts, she had failed to catch up to the main group.

"Interesting garden," she said to herself as she edged her way down the steps. After feeling the trunk of one of the palm trees, she spotted the purple among the glowing yellow flowers. She looked around briefly. Yes, the garden was deserted. She crept closer. "It's been quite a day," she said. "If I want to smell one flower, I will." And she failed to notice twelve handbags half hidden by the carpet of yellow.

Mr Monroe barely touched the wrought iron handrails and smiled. His plan had gone off without a hitch. He rifled through each handbag and pocketed any cash he found there.

One visit to Fay's Garden Delights later, Mr Monroe stepped out of his car with his brand-new flamingo statue.

He couldn't wait to see it in its new home. Right in the centre of the front lawn. He stepped back and admired his purchase. Heroic stance. Noble expression. Sturdily built. It was simply the finest flamingo he had seen.

Pearl's throat was as dry as a sand drift. She had been wandering around the desert landscape for several hours with no water in sight. She looked up at the sky. Dusk was setting in. If she didn't find water soon, she would have to go without until the next morning. Suddenly, she spotted a dot on the horizon and simultaneously heard the thundering of hooves. As the dot neared, she realised it was a cowboy on a horse.

"Howdy, ma'am," he said as he pulled on the reins.

Pearl stared at him. "Where am I?" she said.

"Well, ma'am, you're right where you need to be."

Alice

Hugibert, leaning back in his chair with his arms folded, looked on as his two young granddaughters danced clockwise around the parlour. Although there was a large emerald-encrusted coffee table in the middle of the room, they managed to avoid it and execute each step perfectly. Opposite Hugibert, Mr Lind leant forward in his armchair and studied both girls. With each leap their frilled hems rose simultaneously and created a puff of air as they fell. Because the girls had performed this routine an interminable number of times, their positioning in each lap was identical. So Mr Lind was hit with a gust each time the girls landed before him, causing the rise and fall of his wispy white fringe. Neither he nor Hugibert spoke throughout the performance; the only sounds heard were the squeak of the girls' shoes and the whisper of their dresses rippling in the air.

When the dance concluded, the two men showed their appreciation through applause.

"You have two beautiful granddaughters, Hugibert," Mr Lind said airily after the girls had left the room in order to fetch drinks for them. "They float like feathers."

"Thank you," Hugibert said softly. "I consider grace to be the most important quality a girl can possess. That is why I have encouraged my granddaughters to dance since birth."

Mr Lind nodded. "Splendid. Grace makes a girl sparkle like a diamond."

The two men looked up as the girls returned to the parlour with their drinks. The older one was carrying her grandfather's glass of port, while the younger carried Mr Lind's sherry. A smile of anticipation formed on Mr Lind's face as the younger girl stepped towards him. In the act of handing him the glass, her hand inadvertently brushed his. "What slender fingers you have," he said dreamily. "And such alabaster skin."

The girl smiled shyly and skipped over to her sister, who had taken her place in front of the bay window after presenting the glass of port to her grandfather.

Hugibert moistened his lips with port, leant forward and set his glass on the coffee table. After flashing a look of utmost pride to his youngest granddaughter, he eased back into his customary position and ran his hands up and down the arms of the chair. "I must agree. From the time of her birth her skin has had the appearance of the finest porcelain." He turned his gaze to the older girl. "Just like her sister."

The two girls blushed deeply.

Silence fell upon the parlour, and Mr Lind became aware of the scent of gardenias in the ornate Victorian vase positioned right at the centre of the coffee table. He drank it in. "I adore gardenias," he murmured, breaking the silence. "Whenever I smell them, I am a little boy again." He took a sip of his sherry, exhaled softly and appeared to sink into a malaise.

A Lime, Cherry and Tangerine
Paisley Tie

When the office worker stepped out of his house wearing his lime, cherry and tangerine paisley tie for the first time, he felt an entirely new man. "I'm certainly going to cause a stir at the office," he said to himself as he swung his briefcase into his car. He had spotted the tie while shopping at the local department store with his wife and knew immediately that he had to have it.

"I know it's a bit brighter than I usually wear," he had said to his wife at the time as he dangled it before her eyes. "But it will make me stand out from the crowd."

As he backed out of the driveway, he thought about how the others would react to his fashion choice when he arrived at work that morning. He was sure his colleague Scott would give him a fair ribbing, but he was less certain about how his boss Mr Rouse would react. It could go one of two ways. He could think him a fool and fire him on the spot, or respect him for his new-found individualistic streak and trust him to come up with innovative solutions to complex problems.

"Hello, Paolo!" the office worker said to his colleague upon stepping out of his car which he had manoeuvred into the last remaining park. Paolo could always be counted on to provide an honest opinion about any subject under the sun. "Getting a quick smoke in?"

Paolo bent over double and hacked a cough in reply.

The office worker stood before his sunken-cheeked colleague and waited patiently for him to look up and notice his tie. Regrettably for both parties, Paolo's single cough proceeded to morph into a full-on coughing fit. After waiting several minutes for it to subside, the office worker decided to press on, as he did not wish to be tardy. "See you in the office, Paolo," he said as he patted his co-worker on the back.

As the office worker approached the glass door that served to separate him from his peers, his eyes were drawn to the lime, cherry and tangerine paisley tie in his reflection. It shone out from his chest like a beacon.

He grasped the door handle. The time had come.

Opening the door with a flourish, he was greeted by the sight of his boss in deep conversation with his colleague Antonio. The office worker stood expectantly for several moments until Mr Rouse noticed him. At first his boss's expression was indifferent. Then it was replaced by fear when Mr Rouse glanced down at the lime, cherry and tangerine tie. "Take a seat, Ehrlich, and I'll tell you a story," he said with a slight shake after a long silence. Mr Rouse eyeballed everyone within his radius. "Take a seat, everybody."

Mr Rouse waited patiently until everyone was seated. When there was complete silence, he began.

"Seven years into our marriage, my wife and I found we were no longer attracted to each other. This is not an uncommon phenomenon. If one were to survey all married couples, I am certain one would find that most have faced this hurdle at some stage. What did we do to try and clear this hurdle, you may ask? All manner of things. We had dinner at the restaurant where we had our first rendezvous. We sat by the riverside, noted the lack of marine life and hypothesised that this was due to the pollution from city living. We took a trip to the country and frolicked in dewy meadows. None of these activities served to reignite the spark. In a last-ditch attempt, we paid a visit to the zoo. I must admit I was sceptical. I kept these thoughts to myself, however, as I did not want to risk damaging our relationship further."

"We entered the zoo, having paid our admission fee to a rotund woman in a kiosk, and studied the sign that informed patrons where each species of animal was located. My wife suggested we view the lions first. I was keen on seeing the giraffes before that, but in a spirit of compromise, I agreed we should start with the lions. As we commenced our journey to the lion enclosure, I felt a great apprehension. If the spark between my wife and me was not reignited by the end of the day, our marriage was as good as over."

"The lions were resting when we arrived at the enclosure. In their number was a massive beast with a fearsome mane that I took to be the husband, a smaller beast with no mane that I took to be the wife and a smaller one that I took to be the child. We stood in the crowd and stared at the creatures until a zookeeper entered the enclosure and announced enthusiastically that it was feeding time. The slight, moustached fellow proceeded to throw a large slab of raw meat in the vicinity of the great cats. After eyeing the hunk of flesh, the patriarch suddenly pounced and tore into it with relish, setting off a frenzy of applause in the crowd. I turned to my wife and met her gaze. My heart plummeted as I realised this spectacle had failed to reignite any spark."

"When feeding time was over, we moved on toward the giraffes. I was suddenly overcome by a wave of depression. If the sight of such animal violence could not bring us together, what would? Certainly not the sight of four giraffes standing around doing nothing, as it turned out. After my wife and I had exhausted all talking points about what lay before us, such as how tall the giraffes were and how many spots they had, we set off to explore the rest of the zoo."

"After several decidedly unstimulating hours, we came to the final enclosure, which happened to contain two banana slugs. As we sat down on a bench facing the enclosure, we looked at each other. We opened our mouths together, me to vocalise the obvious and her presumably to do the same, when something extraordinary happened. One of the banana slugs, which had been lolling in the corner, edged over to its fellow captive and began to pulsate. Judging by its body language, the other slug appeared to be receptive. What followed was the most exciting spectacle I have ever witnessed. My wife and I were transfixed. She gripped my hand. We stood up and charged towards the exit."

"Once out, we made for the wood next to the car park and indulged in the same act – watched by birds, squirrels and, eventually, several curious pensioners. We returned home, believing the spark was back. The next morning, however, we found that this was not the case. After laying waste to the back fence with my wellingtons, I came inside and we discussed the possible reasons for our failure. We concluded that the sight of a banana slug embrace was now required as a catalyst for any physical activity between us. In order to test our theory, we decided to return to the zoo."

"Having paid our admission fee to the same rotund woman, we made a beeline for the banana slug enclosure. The two creatures were situated approximately a metre apart and appeared to be asleep – much to our disappointment. My wife and I decided to wait as long as it took for the most sacred of acts to occur. When we took our places on the bench, she took a wrapped chutney sandwich out of her pocket and offered me half. As I was quite peckish, I accepted."

"After several hours I began to worry that we would not see what we had come for. I looked around and noted that visitor attendance was considerably spottier than it had been when we arrived. Suddenly, I felt a sharp nudge in my ribs. I whipped round on my wife and saw where she was pointing. Our glistening friends. Sure enough, what I took to be the male had worked its way over to what I took to be the female and begun to throb as it had the day before. Again, the female appeared receptive. What followed was well and truly worth the wait. I gripped my wife's hand."

"The following day we arrived at the zoo several minutes before opening time. When the kiosk woman slid the window open and saw us, she raised her eyebrows. Undeterred, we paid our admission fee and headed straight for the slugs. As we took our usual positions, I noticed a zookeeper inside the enclosure. I walked up to him and asked the question my wife and I had discussed: were the banana slugs for sale? Much to my disappointment, he told me they were not and laughed heartily at the idea that I would want to buy them."

"Angered, I returned to my spot on the bench and broke the news to my wife. A tear began to snake its way down her cheek, which upset me further. I sat there fuming, while the zookeeper exited the enclosure and headed back down the path we had taken, chuckling to himself."

"My wife turned to me and told me to stay put. She was going to liberate the slugs. I warned her that management would soon identify the culprits, but she waved me off, and sprang to her feet."

"I scanned the surrounding area. Luckily, the banana slug enclosure was as far from the entrance as possible, and there were no patrons about. When my wife reached the top of the wire structure, she threw her hands up and cried to me that we would soon have all we needed, right there at home. What happened next is forever etched in my memory. As she threw her hands up and let go of the wire, she lost her balance and fell into the enclosure headfirst, snapping her neck like a breadstick. I watched in horror and arousal as the banana slugs came together and gave into temptation beside the corpse."

Mr Rouse exhaled and turned back to Antonio. "And if you cannot locate one in the office, you have my permission to buy one from Laird's Office Supplies," he said. "Pay for it out of petty cash."

Extract from
'An Illustrated History of Whitley'

Which leads us to an incident known for evermore as 'That Time Those Idiots Fought Over a Patch of Dirt'. Members of the Strawberry Growers Club were making for a small patch of dirt in the middle of town, right next to that tree with the branches that look like the waving arms of dancers, in order to plant strawberries. What they did not know was that members of the Raspberry Growers Club had that very same patch in their sights.

What followed was a heated confrontation between the two groups. At first, each expressed surprise that the other group had appeared in the same place at the same time. Then, when each learnt of the other group's intentions, angry words were exchanged. When one of the members of the Raspberry Growers Club snatched the straw hat from a member of the Strawberry Growers Club and tossed it away like a frisbee, the situation escalated into violence. The founder of the Strawberry Growers Club began to swing his trowel about, while a member of the Raspberry Growers Club grabbed one of the opposing group members by the overalls and sank her teeth into her neck. Ears were twisted, shins were kicked, and noses blown.

At the height of the violence, members of the Loganberry Growers Club arrived and attempted to pacify members of both groups, having witnessed the scene unfold from their headquarters on the fifth floor of that building that looks like a big face with a hundred eyes. The Loganberry Growers were immediately met with hostility from both groups and found themselves thoroughly battered. Eventually, a large contingent of police arrived on the scene and got the situation under control, but not before one retiree tackled a veterinarian attempting to plant a row of strawberries in all the commotion.

Coffee and Cake

It was mid-afternoon when childhood friends Winifred Barnes and Valerie Knight entered a small café to have coffee and cake. Winifred, a short, plump woman with cropped blonde hair, noticed that the clientele was predominantly younger than her and her middle-aged friend. This was not the case with Valerie, a woman of average height and girth with shoulder-length grey hair. She was too busy looking at the unconventional light fittings to notice the age of the patrons.

The two ladies surveyed the available tables and eventually decided on one in the corner that provided what they considered a nice view of the lake. After they had sat down, Winifred grabbed the menu with her thick bejewelled fingers. She scanned it and settled on a slice of carrot cake and a cappuccino. Valerie nodded, took the menu and scanned it herself. She decided on a slice of lemon cake and a cappuccino. Nodding as she rehearsed their order in silence, she stood up and went to the counter. It was her turn to pay.

While Winifred waited for her to return with their portions of cake, she watched the young people talk and laugh and sip their lattes. It may have been her imagination playing tricks on her, but she got the impression that she and Valerie were not welcome. When Valerie at last set down their cake and their table number, Winifred exhaled silently.

WB: This is a lovely setting.

VK: I know.

WB: I could sit here and watch those sailboats all day.

VK: So could I.

WB: I've never been on a sailboat, have you?

VK: Never.

WB: I wonder what it feels like. I don't think I'd like it all that much. It's supposed to be a bit bumpy, isn't it?

VK: Yes. David went on one of those boats – oh, it must have been nearly five years ago now. And he said it was a bit bumpy.

WB: I'm not surprised.

VK: Yes.

WB: How is David going?

VK: Oh, he's going all right. You know David.

WB: Yes.

VK: Yes.

WB: Does he still work for that man who's married to – what's her name?

VK: Wilson Davis?

WB: No, it started with an 'I', I think.

VK: Oh, Ingrid.

WB: Yes. Ingrid Davis.

VK: No, he doesn't work for him anymore. He wanted more money than he was prepared to pay, so he asked for a job at another firm.

WB: Oh. Did he get it?

VK: Yes.

WB: That's good.

VK: Yes.

WB: And how's Melissa?

VK: Oh, she's good. You know Melissa.

WB: Yes.

VK: Yes.

WB: Does she still work for the Water Board?

VK: Oh, yes, in fact she —

A young blonde waitress suddenly appeared at their table with the coffees. "Two cappuccinos?" she said perkily.

"Yes, thank you," Valerie said as the waitress placed a mug in front of each of them.

"Thank you," Winifred said to her back as she departed with their table number.

WB: You were saying about Melissa.

VK: Yes. She works for the Water Board.

WB: Yes.

VK: Hmm.

Valerie sipped her cappuccino while Winifred shovelled a forkful of carrot cake into her mouth. After turning it over with her tongue an inordinate number of times, she finally swallowed it and leant in closer.

WB: And how's little Bobbi?

VK: Oh, she's a little darling. You know Bobbi.

WB: No, I don't.

VK: You've never met Bobbi?

WB: No.

VK: Really?

WB: No.

VK: Well. I'll have to ask Melissa to come with me next time and have her bring little Bobbi. She's a sweetheart.

WB: Is she?

VK: Yes. She's just started to walk.

WB: Really?

VK: Yes. She certainly keeps her mummy and daddy on their toes.

WB: Well, if she's walking, she would!

VK: I know.

Winifred sighed and leant back in her chair.

WB: It doesn't seem that long ago that Melissa was pregnant. And now —

VK: I know.

WB: Now she's walking.

VK: Yes.

Winifred rested her fork on the plate and looked at the table. She was not feeling the best. Trying to take her mind off the situation, she focused on a stain on the tablecloth. As Valerie stirred her cappuccino, Winifred felt her nausea disappear, only to be replaced by some sort of tickling. The sensation moved upwards into her throat.

Her head began to shake violently. As Valerie stirred her cappuccino, an enormous purple mass erupted from Winifred's mouth and hit the table with a wet thump. A scream from one of the patrons rang out around the café. Winifred dabbed at her lips with a serviette. The purple mass thrashed around on the table until it tumbled onto the floor and scuttled toward two young women, who shrieked and ran out of the café without finishing their lattes.

VK: So, how's George?

WB: Oh, he's as active as ever. I told him the other day that he ought to be slowing down at his age – at *our* age – but do you think he listened?

Valerie shook her head.

WB: He just went on another walk. I tell you, he just seems to be going on more and more walks!

VK: Well, he's always loved nature, hasn't he?

WB: Yes. When I first met him, he had a bird on his shoulder.

VK: Really?

WB: Yes, really! One of those beautiful red and green parrots.

VK: Oh, I love those. I remember one used to visit us and splash around in our birdbath. I haven't seen it lately, though.

WB: No?

VK: No.

Winifred deposited the rest of the carrot cake in her mouth.

WB: This is quite nice, Valerie.

VK: It looks quite nice. I haven't had carrot cake for a long time.

WB: It's my favourite.

VK: Really?

WB: Yes, ever since I was a little girl.

VK: Really? I can't say I've ever been a huge fan of carrot cake. I've always been partial to lemon cake.

WB: I love lemon cake.

VK: So do I.

Valerie picked up her slice of lemon cake and took a bite.

WB: That looks nice.

VK: Hmm. I've had better.

WB: Really?

VK: Yes.

Valerie tilted her head slightly.

VK: The icing doesn't taste quite right.

WB: Oh, that's a shame.
VK: Yes.

Valerie picked up the rest of her cake and stuffed it in her mouth.

WB: A lemon cake must have good icing.
VK: I know.
WB: Hmm.
VK: Thankfully, the cappuccino is nice.
WB: That's the main thing.
VK: Absolutely.

The young waitress was back, but not so perky this time. She glanced at Winifred, took the two empty plates and disappeared without a word. As Winifred watched her depart, she again felt a pang of nausea. Instinctively, she clutched her stomach, which did not quell the discomfort. That tickling sensation returned and snaked its way up to her throat.

Winifred's head jerked back and forth until another purple object burst from her mouth and hit the table. This one was even larger than the first. After several moments of lying still, the creature began to writhe. Valerie grabbed her serviette, wiped the slimy film off the rim of her mug and finished her cappuccino as the creature fell off the table and plopped onto the floor.

WB: Yes, a café has to serve a decent cappuccino.
VK: Yes.

The waitress returned, picked up the two empty mugs and left.

VK: Well, that was nice. I'll have to remember to ask Melissa to come next time and bring Bobbi. She's a beautiful girl. A real free spirit.

WB: She sounds lovely.

VK: She is.

WB: It doesn't surprise me. Her parents are such nice people.

VK: Yes, they are. We were so happy when David married Melissa.

WB: Oh, I can imagine.

VK: Yes. They're a lovely couple.

WB: Yes. I remember —

Mid-sentence Winifred was seized by a familiar feeling. She waited for the inevitable tickling – and there it was. Nothing to do now but anticipate the climb. This time Valerie watched calmly as a multitude of legs poked out from between Winifred's lips and thrashed about in the air. She became concerned, however, when her friend began to choke.

Valerie got to her feet as quickly as her engorged state allowed, walked around behind Winifred's chair and slapped her friend on the back. This appeared to do the trick. Winifred's head lurched forward and three massive slime-covered creatures fell out of her mouth in a tangled heap. With café patrons screaming, the three creatures bounced wetly off the table and onto the floor. After thrashing about briefly, they got their bearings and scuttled off in separate directions.

A man who the two ladies took to be the owner of the café strode up to their table, glowering. "I'm afraid I'm going to have to ask you to leave, ladies," he snapped. "I think you know why."

Winifred turned to Valerie. "I knew we weren't welcome here," she said. "I knew it from the moment we walked in. This is a young person's café." The two women grabbed their purses and headed for the door.

A Short Essay on the
Positive and Negative Aspects
of the Hallway

One of the most useful domestic spaces is the hallway. Comprising a floor, at least two walls and a ceiling, the hallway serves to connect the main section of the house to the rooms that branch off to the side. At once imposing and inviting, its simple design allows for ease of entry and exit, provided one possesses satisfactory motor skills. The hallway is also typically straight, thus allowing for high visibility of predators and hence low probability of death. There is an exception to this rule, however, as some hallways meander, resulting in low general visibility and increased probability of unseen predators. Nevertheless, such hallways are few and far between, so it is ultimately unlikely that one would meet one's end in the space in question.

It is not just functionality that has cemented the hallway's reputation as one of our most beloved spaces. Flexibility also plays a key role. One notable example of this is the opportunity afforded the owner to transform the hallway into a seemingly different space through the use of accessories such as the hallway runner. Typically spanning the full length, the hallway runner comes in a variety of colours and can transform the space into anything from a slice of the orient to a tropical paradise.

While the hallway runner can bring great joy to the user, it should be noted that it can also bring considerable risk. If one were to slip on the runner while in progress down the hallway, serious injury might occur, the severity of which would depend on the angle at which one hits the floor and the heaviness of the fall. While the vast majority of injuries incurred in this manner could be classified as low level, such as sprained ankles or grazed knees, there have been instances in which high level injuries have been sustained, such as broken bones and, in rare cases, dislodged heads.

The installation of light fixtures can also transform a hallway from dark and forbidding to a light, welcoming space. However, like hallway runners, light fixtures also pose potential problems. While they provide much needed light for night-time locomotion, they also have the propensity to fall at random times, obliterating any individual who happens to be walking underneath them. One must weigh up the advantages of entering a well-lit hallway with the disadvantages of possible extinction before one decides to proceed. Of course, if one makes the decision to remove all light fixtures, this leaves one vulnerable to the threat of ever-present predators, not to mention injury if one comes into contact with a wall during a night-time stroll.

In summary, the hallway is a functional and flexible domestic space. But one must be prepared for danger before venturing into it. Provided one keeps one's wits about one, however, the hallway poses no greater threat to one's life than the bedroom with its tilting wardrobe or the kitchen with its exploding stove.

El Fotógrafo de Queso

An explosion of light temporarily filled the room. The moment it disappeared, another explosion took its place and disappeared as quickly as the first. Slowly, an old woman emerged from underneath a black shroud that was connected to a camera that rested on a tripod. She made her way over to a table on which a block of gruyère cheese was placed three centimetres to the left of a block of stilton. After contemplating the blocks for a moment, she reached out a withered hand and turned the block of gruyère forty-five degrees counterclockwise. With this, she turned, shuffled back to the camera and resumed her position. Again, an explosion of light rocketed into the walls, followed by two more in quick succession. The old woman drew the shroud across her silver hair and shuffled back to the table.

This time she picked up the block of stilton and balanced it carefully on top of the gruyère. She checked the scene through the viewfinder, returned to the table and made an adjustment, then once again resumed her position behind the camera and took two photographs. As the light disappeared into nothingness, the old woman shuffled into her kitchen and re-emerged with a moderate-sized wedge of brie. After much thought, she placed the brie directly in front of the block of gruyère on which the block of stilton had been placed, with the point of the wedge facing to the right. Moments after she slipped back under the shroud, the room was bathed in light once more.

The Alpaca

"Any croquembouche?" In the wake of this question, a tear began to roll down Simon's cheek. His wife Nava shot him a pleading glance from the chair opposite, as if the slight, bespectacled man of forty-one possessed the ability to reverse its descent.

"No, Father," Nava said softly. Gus, a bent-over, portly man of eighty-six, had just finished his portion of the curry that his daughter Nava, a towering, raven-haired woman of forty-three, had prepared in their farmhouse kitchen. He had expected an imminent progression to the next course and was surprised to find that this would not occur.

It was the brusque tone Gus had used while addressing Nava, coupled with a particularly stressful day at work, that had led to Simon breaking down at this seemingly innocuous question. When Gus heard the answer, he glared at his daughter, quickly stuffed his mouth with every morsel of curry that was left in the serving pot and leant back in his chair. All was still until Simon stood up abruptly and wiped his eyes with his napkin, which he had momentarily forgotten he had used. After flicking a squashed pea off his eyebrow, he let out a shriek and rushed off in the direction of the bedroom he shared with his wife. Father and daughter sat in silence for several moments until Nava excused herself.

Nava sat next to her husband on the bed as he wept into her bosom.

"I'm sorry," he said, wiping the tears and remnants of curry out of his eyes. "I try not to react, but sometimes I just can't help it."

"It's okay," Nava cooed as she tried to brush the partly chewed carrot off the front of her dress without her husband noticing.

"I suppose I should go and apologise," Simon said softly, after he had settled down. "It can't be easy for him." He stared into space for several moments.

"Still, he shouldn't treat you that way." Nava sighed.

"He's always treated me that way, darling. He treated my mother the same. But she loved him, and I promised her that I would take care of him after she was gone, so that's what I'm going to do."

Simon returned to the dining room, where Gus remained in his chair. Simon placed a hand on the elderly man's shoulder. "I'm sorry about my outburst, Gus," he said. "I've had a long day. Can you forgive me?"

Gus sat motionless for an inordinate length of time, then slowly raised his head to meet Simon's gaze. His lips parted as if he were about to speak, then the contents of his mouth came tumbling out, helped by a shrivelled tongue in a scene not unlike the birth of a mammal. As Simon looked down in horror at the mush on the back of his hand, Gus's lips formed a sneer.

It had been a year since Simon and Nava moved into their farmhouse. Upon their arrival in the country, they managed to secure the relatively well-paying jobs of financial planner and veterinarian respectively and planned to put aside some of the money they earned so Nava could buy the alpaca she had always wanted. However, not a month after they moved in, Nava's mother passed away after a brief but courageous battle with her neighbour's Yorkshire terrier, leaving her father alone in the city apartment they had shared for almost sixty years. Despite some trepidation from both parties, it was decided that Nava's father would move into the farmhouse, owing to the fact that he could not attend satisfactorily to his physical ailments, which included high blood pressure, low earlobes, gout, a temperamental incus, a rapidly expanding waistline and general decrepitude.

Consequently, Nava relinquished her position of veterinarian at the local clinic so she could dedicate herself to the full-time care of her father, a decision that meant giving up her dream of owning an alpaca due to the subtraction of half the family's income and the additional cost of her father's upkeep. Often Nava would gaze out of the kitchen window and imagine an alpaca frolicking in the empty paddock.

However, these dreams would be shattered regularly by the voice of her father calling out to her to wash his feet or perform some such task.

One particularly warm summer night, Gus was seated in his favourite armchair in the left-hand corner of the living room with his daughter bent over him, trimming his eyebrows. Simon was seated on the right side of the couch not far from the armchair, with his hand placed on the left side, which was still warm from his wife sitting there earlier. As usual, the family were watching a western, as Gus was a devoted fan of the genre. Once Nava had finished her duty, Gus allowed her to rejoin her husband on the couch.

On the screen the hero rode up to a farm owned by the villain, who came out of the house firing. Gus cackled.

"That looks like our house," Simon said, trying to engage Gus in conversation, despite there being little resemblance.

As hero and villain traded shots, Gus turned to Simon with a grin and said "It can't be. I see an alpaca."

Simon seethed, but said nothing.

When the hero turned the wounded villain over to the local sheriff, Gus let out a loud groan.

"What's wrong, Father?" Nava said, rushing over.

"My belly hurts. Rub it." Gus lifted his dirty yellow polo shirt to reveal his stomach, which was becoming dangerously large.

She began to rub it immediately. It was like a beach ball, coated in perspiration, owing to both the heat and the thrilling nature of the film. Gus groaned again. Simon kept his eyes on the screen, doing his best to ignore the situation.

"My back hurts," Gus moaned. "I want to go to bed."

Nava helped her father carefully to his feet before Simon reluctantly got up and came over to help.

"Don't touch me," Gus spat as Simon tried to grab his right arm. As the credits began to roll, Nava walked her father to his room. Simon looked on, utterly helpless.

That night in bed Simon had a phone call from his boss, telling him that his presence would be required at a conference from Wednesday to Friday the following week. As it was being held out of town, Simon would have to stay at a hotel for its duration. He glanced at Nava, then reluctantly told his boss that he would be there. He hung up the phone and let out a protracted sigh. "If you didn't pick that up, I have to go to a conference next week," he said.

Nava shrugged. "Well – if you have to go, you have to go," she said.

"I know." Simon winced. "It's just that I hate leaving you to look after your father on your own. It's getting to be a pretty difficult job."

When it came time for Simon to leave for the conference, he was torn. He was desperately looking forward to getting away from Gus, but at the same time felt exceedingly guilty about leaving his wife alone with her father. By this time, Gus's stomach had become so sizeable that if he fell, it was unlikely Nava would be able to get him to his feet. His various ailments were also giving him so much trouble that he was in constant pain. Simon began to fear that if Gus did fall and Nava did attempt to pick him up, he might lash out at her.

"Goodbye, Gus," he said to the old man, who had sunk deeper into his favourite armchair. "Be sure to do what your daughter says."

Gus bared his tobacco-stained teeth at Simon and returned to his newspaper.

"Bye, honey," Simon said, turning to Nava.

"Goodbye, darling." She wrapped her arms around her husband. "Have a nice time."

Four days later Simon pulled into his driveway, whistling. He had enjoyed his time away immensely and was the calmest he had been since his father-in-law moved in. As he got out of the car and began to walk toward the farmhouse with his suitcase, he noticed Nava crouched over Gus under the apple tree in the side garden. With his curiosity piqued, he set down his suitcase and wandered over. He noticed immediately that both were in a state of acute distress.

"Oh, Simon," Nava cried, "Father was in the garden stomping on the daisies when his stomach started to hurt and he had to lie down. That was this morning. Oh, Simon, what do we do? I think he's dying." She gripped her father's hand as he let out a thundering bellow.

Simon and Nava fixed their eyes on Gus's stomach, which was heaving violently. Simon tried his best to think of a solution but somehow couldn't kick his brain into gear.

The husband and wife looked on in horror as Gus's waters broke and a cascade of fluid flowed forth. Simon put his hand over his mouth and Nava let out a deafening scream as a glistening white leg burst out of Gus and into the summer air. Nava kept screaming as another leg appeared, followed by a tail. By this time, Simon was lying unconscious on the grass. Nava took one look at him. It was up to her to deliver her father's offspring. She braced herself, grabbed the pair of slippery legs and yelled at her father to push. No response. So she pulled with all her might and the beast slid out of her father with surprising ease. Exhausted, she examined the creature. It was a perfectly formed baby alpaca.

It Snows Up in Snow Country

As the train approached the station, I looked around the place where I had been sitting for any litter as per the announcement. When I was satisfied there was none, and that I had deposited it all in the bin at the end of the carriage, I sat and stared at the back of the seat in front of me. The train would soon be at the station and it would be up to me to find my way to Harold's Ski Lodge. Not my grandmother. Me. I felt nervous but also confident that I was up to the task. After all, I had almost navigated my way from the first station to the last.

"Mount Gaggle Station. Final stop. Thank you for travelling with us and we hope you have a lovely day."

I sprang to my feet and picked up my bag. After waiting for everyone to exit the train, I headed out and was hit with a blast of cold air. I zipped up my ski jacket and looked for a sign telling me where I could find Harold's Ski Lodge. No sign. I looked around for someone who might know and decided on a squat woman with kind eyes.

"Excuse me, miss," I said. "Would you by any chance know where Harold's Ski Lodge is?"

She looked up at me and giggled. "No!" she said mischievously and danced away. I looked around for someone more stable and decided on a man of average height with a hen on his head.

"Excuse me, sir," I said. "Would you by any chance know where I could find Harold's Ski Lodge?" The man looked up – I hoped in thought. After several moments, he reached up and took the hen off his head, revealing a freshly laid egg. He took the egg and handed it to me.

"May your yolk never run," he said solemnly. I thanked him and looked for anyone else I could ask.

I spotted a man in a uniform. "Excuse me, sir," I said as I approached him. "Are you a station worker?"

"Oh, no," he said. "I wear this uniform for fun."

"Oh," I said. "I might ask someone else, then."

"Ask them what?"

"How to get to Harold's Ski Lodge," I said.

His face lit up. "I can tell you how to get there." He was excited. "You see that building over there?"

I nodded.

"It's to the right of that."

"Thank you." I handed him my egg and set off.

One short walk later, I was at Harold's Ski Lodge. Upon entering I was greeted by the sight of a woman in a floral dress pocketing money from a cash register. She was heavily tanned, a fact I found incomprehensible as this was snow country.

"Hello," I said tentatively. "This is Harold's Ski Lodge, isn't it?"

The woman smiled. "I'm afraid Harold's Ski Lodge is closed for the time being," she said.

"Why?" I said, shocked.

"Harold's dead." She pressed her lips together.

The woman resumed raiding the till. Suddenly I was struck by the fact that I would have to find another place to stay. "Uh – where shall I go then?" I said.

She looked me up and down. "How old are you?" she said.

"I'm fourteen, miss," I said. "Well, fourteen and a half, and I've come up for the school holidays to learn how to ski."

She appeared to think briefly. "I'll tell you what," she said. "How about you come and stay with me and my husband? We've got enough space."

So began my two-week stay with Mr and Mrs Neck.

"It's awfully nice to meet you, lad," said Mr Neck after his wife had filled him in on the reason a fourteen-year-old boy was standing in his living room. "If you want skiing you've come to the right place. I don't ski myself and neither does my wife, but you're bound to find someone in town willing to teach you."

"Thank you, Mr Neck," I said. "It's very nice of you to let me stay here."

"Think nothing of it, lad," he said, waving a hand in the air. "We have more than enough space."

I spent most of the afternoon in the living room talking with him. As it turned out, he usually commuted to the city on weekdays, but had taken the day off upon learning of the death of his neighbour, Harold. I asked Mr Neck where he worked.

"It's a large business, lad. The largest of its kind in the southern hemisphere."

"What is it?" I said.

He grinned. "It's a large business, lad. The largest of its kind in the southern hemisphere."

"Yes, but what do you do there?"

His grin grew wider. "Business."

Clearly, for one reason or another, Mr Neck was not about to tell me what he did for a living.

Mrs Neck emerged from the kitchen and asked me if I would like to help her prepare dinner. "We're having an extra special feast tonight," she said.

I followed her into the kitchen.

I was confronted with a room that was slightly larger than normal, which surprised me as the other rooms I had seen were slightly smaller than normal. I was also confronted by the naked corpse of an elderly man laid out on the kitchen island. Mrs Neck caught the expression of surprise on my face.

"We wanted a large kitchen, so we had to make the other rooms smaller," she explained. "Otherwise, the house wouldn't have fit on the lot." I nodded and asked what I could do to help with dinner.

"You can chop up some potatoes for me if you'd like," she said. "You'll find them in the pantry on the shelf second from the bottom."

Mr Neck burst into the kitchen with a grin on his face. "Helping out with dinner, lad?" he said. "Good boy." He turned to the corpse. "Ah, Harold is ready for the pot." Then he turned to me and leant in close. So close, I could smell the cigar smoke on his breath. "We don't waste anything up here, lad. If something falls into our lap, we use it."

I nodded. "I'm going to chop up the potatoes," I said.

"Ah," Mr Neck said absentmindedly. He turned to his wife. "Has he been tenderized?"

She nodded.

The grin returned to her husband's face. "Good."

He turned to me and pointed to the corpse. "This one's been pre-felled. Not by me, not by my wife, but by a higher being." He leant in toward me again. "If it has to be done, I'm not above carrying out the felling." He waited several moments before resuming his customary straight-backed stance.

"I might get started with the potatoes, Mr Neck," I said quietly.

After dinner I excused myself from the table in order to go to bed. "Goodnight, lad!" Mr Neck said as he dabbed at some sauce trailing out of the corner of his mouth. "Have a good rest."

"Yes, have a good rest," added Mrs Neck. "You've had a long journey." I smiled and left the room as Mr Neck spat out what appeared to be gristle.

The following morning I got up early so I would have an abundance of time to look for a ski instructor. After zipping up my ski jacket, I said goodbye to my hosts and stepped out into the blistering cold air. The town was mine!

First, I went straight to the town square. No ski instructor among the tourists there. I caught the chairlift up to the top of Mount Gaggle. No ski instructor there, either. So I rode back down to the foot of the mountain and wandered in no particular direction.

After about a ten-minute walk through a forest I came to a small clearing with a picnic table in the centre of it. Someone must have placed it there, hoping that the snow would clear, and it would be a pleasant spot for a picnic. With its view of the lake (although frozen over right now), it seemed that I was right. I dumped my bag on the table and sat down.

I was almost fully rested when a girl with a long blonde ponytail skied past. Excited, I bounced up and ran out of the clearing. Maybe she was a ski instructor.

I watched until she was almost out of sight. I did not have the courage to call out to her to come back, but luckily, she did anyway. As she got closer, I noticed how pretty she was.

"Hello," I said after she came to a stop. "You ski well."

She laughed. "I guess so."

My mouth suddenly felt like a desert. "So – do you live here?" I managed to ask.

"Yeah," she said. "All my life."

"I see." I stared at her for several moments until I remembered to ask her if she could teach me how to ski.

"Do you have any skis?" she said.

I looked down. I was wearing hiking boots. "I guess not," I said.

"Well," she smiled, "you're going to need skis."

I could feel my face getting hot. "I suppose it will be a bit late by the time I go and rent some," I said.

She shrugged. "We could start tomorrow if you'd like."

I nodded. "That would be great. Up at the summit? Don't worry – I'll make sure I bring skis."

She nodded and skied off. "What's your name?" I called out after her.

"Gabrielle!" she shouted without even glancing over her shoulder.

I got back to Mr and Mrs Neck's house just in time for dinner. Mrs Neck had prepared cheese and onion pie, a more normal meal than the night before.

"Welcome home, lad!" Mr Neck said as I joined him at the dining table. "Did you have a good day?"

"Actually a great day, Mr Neck. I met a girl and she's going to teach me how to ski."

He grinned and craned his neck toward the kitchen. "Did you hear that? Romance is in the air!"

My face felt all hot again. "It's not a romance, Mr Neck. She's just going to teach me how to ski."

He laughed and set his jowls rippling. "Oh, that's what they all say." He winked.

His expression suddenly changed, and he leant forward. "Say, could you do me a favour, lad? A white goes nicely with cheese and onion pie. Could you go down to the cellar and bring one back? The door's at the end of the hallway."

Now it was my turn to smile. "No problem. My grandmother's got a cellar and I'm always fetching wine for her, so I know what's what."

I headed down the dark, seemingly never-ending hallway. Finally, I came to a heavy wooden door. I opened it and found myself at the top of a flight of immaculate concrete steps, not at all like the crumbling concrete steps you see in horror films. When I looked down, the wine racks lined the far wall from floor to ceiling.

After dinner we relocated to the living room, Mr Neck still with glass in hand. I started toward one of the armchairs but he asked me to join him and his wife on the couch. His words were slightly slurred. As I sat down, he placed his glass on the coffee table and lit a cigar. I choked as he exhaled, but he didn't seem to notice.

"Now tell me about your hopes and dreams, lad," he said, turning to me. I did not know quite what to say.

"I don't know if I've got any," I said.

He let out a great belly laugh. "Everyone has hopes and dreams." He turned back to his wife. "My dream was to find the perfect woman. I didn't achieve it – but I came close." He laughed again and took the cigar out of his mouth.

All was quiet until smacking sounds filled the room. I turned and saw that Mr Neck had deposited his tongue down his wife's throat. I concluded that our conversation was over and headed for my bedroom.

I got up early again the next morning and headed for a ski rental place I had seen in the town square the day before. I wanted to get in early so I would not be late for my lesson. After renting the skis in addition to the rest of the equipment, I headed for the summit of Mount Gaggle. On the way I began to worry that my new friend would not be there. I imagined her sitting at home picturing me alone on Mount Gaggle with only my skis for company. Before I knew it, I felt myself getting all hot again.

I need not have worried.

"Ready for your lesson?" she said brightly when I arrived. I managed to tell her that I was, despite the lump in my throat. The following three hours or so proved physically strenuous, but enjoyable because I was getting to know Gabrielle. As we parted, I tried to kiss her hand, but failed because I was wearing a helmet and she a glove.

When I neared the house, I noticed a steady stream of dishevelled people exiting, including one heavily tanned man with an open shirt and gold chain draped around his neck. Upon passing the letterbox three withered women emerged from the house and congregated around me.

"Ooh, you're a handsome boy," the first one said.

"Isn't he just," cooed the second.

"I could just wrap him up and take him home," the third woman said as she pinched my cheeks. I wormed my way out of their clutches, raced into the house and inadvertently landed in the arms of Mrs Neck.

"Sorry, Mrs Neck," I said as I got my bearings.

"Oh, that's quite all right," she said with a laugh. "I see you met the Gripley triplets. They were here for the party that's just finished up." I nodded and headed to my room. To my surprise Mr Neck was sitting on my bed, struggling to put his shirt on.

"Hello, lad," he said cheerfully. I stared at his almost translucent flesh darting every which way as he struggled. He had worked up quite a sweat in the attempt. Finally, he managed to slide both his arms into the sleeves and began the process of buttoning up. "Make any progress on the skiing?"

I nodded.

"And in other areas?" He smirked.

"I'm fully focused on the skiing, Mr Neck," I said.

He laughed to himself. "I'm sure you are, lad."

The next morning I met Gabrielle at our usual place. She was wearing a pink and grey ski jacket.

"Hello, Gabrielle," I said. "You look particularly fetching."

She burst out laughing. "Is that the best you've got?"

I bowed my head. "Sorry," I said sadly. She kept laughing and motioned for me to follow her. I clomped along for several metres.

"You'll be gliding by the end of the week," she said with a smile.

That prediction turned out to be true, as I was indeed gliding by Sunday.

"Look at you!" she said as I whizzed past. Unfortunately, I overestimated my abilities and found my braking skills were not as developed as my gliding.

I ended up in a heap on the snow.

I said goodbye to Gabrielle and went back to the house that had become my home over the past week and to the two people who had become like parents. Thoughts of Gabrielle ran wild in my head.

Mr and Mrs Neck were in their bedroom getting ready for what appeared to be an outing.

"Hello, lad!" Mr Neck said. "We're just about to go down to the town square. You can come along if you like." I was tired, but I decided to join in, as I wanted to be polite.

On the way we talked about my late mother and father. While it was painful reliving my grief, it did help.

As soon as we reached the town square Mr Neck began to take his clothes off. I looked on as he flung the last of his modesty away and posed like a star.

"Proceed with the flogging, dear," he said in a loud,

clear voice. Mrs Neck produced a sizeable whip from her bag. I looked around at the passers-by. As nobody seemed particularly interested, I gathered that this was just a normal Sunday. Mrs Neck turned side on, planted her feet in the snow, drew her arm back and proceeded to let her husband have it.

"Arghhh!" he shouted after the whip lashed his bare back. "That's the ticket!" he added.

Mrs Neck repeated the action and produced another cry of pain.

The flogging continued for as long as Mr Neck was physically able to withstand it. When it was over, his back was in such a state that he really ought to have had medical attention. After he had got dressed, he turned to me with a broad smile.

"Punishment for the sins we commit throughout the week, lad. Every Sunday my wife and I come down here and engage in this ritual."

I nodded and watched Mrs Neck take her clothes off and hand him the whip.

"Want to have the first crack, lad?" Mr Neck said. I shook my head. He took up the whipping position. "Ready, dear?"

"Yes!" Mrs Neck said eagerly.

Over the next few days, I continued to develop my skiing skills and my relationship with Gabrielle also progressed. By the time Friday rolled around, we had got to holding hands. My joy was tempered, however, by the fact that our time together was coming to an end.

"How am I supposed to go back and focus on schoolwork?" I said. "Without you?"

"We can write to each other," she offered.

I sighed. "It just won't be the same."

The following morning at the breakfast table Mr Neck told me that he and his wife were planning an extra special feast that night because it was my last night at Mount Gaggle.

"That's so kind of you," I said. "I should be serving *you* a special feast."

Mr Neck shook his head and set those jowls going again. "The pleasure has been all ours, lad," he said. He shovelled a spoonful of porridge into his mouth and stared into space. "The end is the toughest part."

I agreed that goodbyes were difficult and excused myself from the table. Speaking of goodbyes, I was now going to have to say the most difficult goodbye of my life.

When I got to the top of the mountain, I couldn't see Gabrielle anywhere. I thought back to the day before. I was sure we hadn't decided to meet at a different time or at a different location. I watched the skiers and began to worry that I wouldn't have a chance to say goodbye to Gabrielle. Before too long, however, I noticed her in the distance. She was moving slower than usual as she was carrying extra skis.

"Sorry I'm late," she said, panting. She dumped the skis on the snow. "They're yours."

"Really?" I couldn't believe it. "You bought them for me?"

She shook her head. "Nah. They're my old skis."

"Oh," I said. "Well thank you, anyway."

Throughout our last session together I tried to keep my focus on the task at hand, but my mind kept wandering. As a result, I didn't make much progress. When we had finished we took off our helmets and goggles. I tried in vain to think of something to say.

"Well, I guess this is it," she said.

I couldn't bear it any longer. I leant forward, kissed her on the lips and fled.

"You forgot your skis!" she shouted after me. I stopped and skulked back, attempting to hide my tear-stained face.

"Sorry about that," I said.

"I forgive you," she said.

After my faux pas we were able to say a proper goodbye, after which I collected my skis.

"Write!" Gabrielle called as she disappeared into the distance.

I got back to Mr and Mrs Neck's house, thoroughly depressed.

"Never mind, lad!" Mr Neck said brightly after I explained my low mood. He whispered like a conspirator, "Just think of tonight's extra special feast. That will take your mind off your girl."

I wandered into the living room and sank into one of the armchairs. I did not mean to, but I fell asleep. Several hours later I was woken by Mr Neck calling my name. I yawned, slowly pulled myself out of the armchair and walked towards his voice. He was in the kitchen with his wife. They shared a glance as I entered.

"Hello, lad," he said softly. "I was wondering if you wouldn't mind fetching me a nice red from the cellar."

As I stepped onto the floor of the cellar, I heard the door click. I turned around and there was Mr Neck at the top of the stairs with what appeared to be a carving knife in his right hand. "Hello, lad!" he said. "Don't mind me. I'm just coming to fell tonight's dinner."

I nodded and started to look for the right bottle of red. Eventually I picked out a fine example and handed it to him. "This should be a good drop," I said.

"Good choice, lad," he said. When he swung the knife and accidentally obliterated one of his prized bottles, I realised what was on the menu. I sprinted up the steps, down the hallway and into my room. I grabbed the skis and bolted for the front door.

"Don't fear the knife, lad!" Mr Neck was shouting not far behind me. I quickly fitted my skis and launched into the night air.

As I practically flew to the station, I could not help feeling slightly betrayed. I thought I had cultivated a positive relationship with Mr and Mrs Neck. But to keep myself from getting unnecessarily upset, I decided to look at the experience from a different point of view. I had learnt a valuable lesson: things are not always as they seem.

Just as I had calmed down, I realised this could also apply to my relationship with Gabrielle. Was this not as it seemed? By the time I reached the platform I was again depressed. Would Gabrielle have tried to murder and devour me eventually? Could I trust anyone in this world? And why was Mr Neck in the midst of dressing when I arrived home after his and his wife's party? These questions and more raced around my head as I boarded the night train home.

Edith's New Hat

"Well if it isn't Noel and Judy! I didn't think you two would make it." John stepped aside to let them enter the house.

"Of course we made it!" Judy said as John kissed her cheek and took her coat. "Not even a hurricane would have stopped us from coming tonight."

"Absolutely," Noel added. "We had to be here to support our friend." Noel and Judy were the kind of couple who appeared to be joined at the hip. So much so, that if one saw either of them out and about on their own, one got a jolt.

"So how have you been?" said John.

Noel and Judy began to answer at the same time, then looked at each other and chuckled. Noel rubbed his moustache and gestured for his wife to answer.

"We've been good, thank you, John," she said, smiling.

John led the way into the living room, which was populated with people of all ages. Noel and Judy glanced at a makeshift curtain that had been erected at the front of the room.

"When will Leo be arriving, John?" asked June, a ruddy-faced woman with large orange earrings.

"Shouldn't be too long now," John replied. "June, do you know Noel and Judy?" June shook her head and walked off.

After discussing the weather briefly with Noel and Judy, John excused himself and headed to the back of the room, where several of Leo's old friends were sitting in their wheelchairs.

"Hello, John," Edith said as she adjusted her new hat. "I'm so looking forward to seeing Leo perform again."

"So am I, Edith," John replied.

"You're a good boy for doing this, John," Frank added. "Getting him back to doing what he loves."

John nodded. "Thanks, Frank," he said. "It's the least I can do after all he's done for me. I couldn't have asked for a better father-in-law." Frank smiled serenely.

Upon hearing a click at the front door, John excused himself and briskly made his way down the hall to greet the arrivals. His wife entered holding onto her father Leo, who in turn was holding onto his ventriloquist's dummy, Archibald.

"Leo," John said warmly as he placed both hands on Leo's shoulders. "I hope you and Archibald are ready. There's a full house." Leo winced slightly. He was wearing his old tuxedo, yet he did not seem like his old self. "Are you feeling all right, Leo?" John frowned.

Leo nodded. "Just my first performance without Doris," he said softly.

John patted Leo on the arm. "She'll be watching from above."

John bounced into the living room and took his place in front of the curtain. "Ladies and gentlemen," he began. "As we all know, our special guest has not had the best time of it recently." He glanced at his wife. "So it is my sincere hope that tonight's proceedings will raise his spirits. Without any further ado, help me welcome Leo and his friend Archibald!" John ran to the side of the curtain, pulled wildly on a rope, and revealed Leo on a stool with Archibald propped on his knee. Hearty applause rang throughout the room.

Instead of launching into his routine, the aged ventriloquist stared at the floor before him. The applause died down and was replaced by a suspenseful silence. Two children began a conversation which was cut short by the swift intervention of their parents.

Leo continued to stare at the floor. A worried look came over John's face. Hesitantly, he began to make his way toward Leo. Leo sat up straight and tried to get himself together, upon which John retreated. Leo adjusted Archibald on his knee and looked up and faced the audience.

"Hello, Archibald," he said, looking at the dummy. "It's been a – it's been —" He stopped and looked at the floor again. His daughter tried but failed to catch his eye with a reassuring glance. Slowly, Leo raised his head. "Long time since —" He stopped again and shifted on his stool. Someone in the audience began to clap in the hope that this would spur him on. It did not.

After several minutes, Leo tried to speak. Nothing came out. Following this, he stared into space.

"Do it for Doris," someone said from the back of the room. This was too much for the elderly man to handle, and he broke down. As the tears flowed, Archibald continued to grin at the audience, oblivious of his friend's anguish. Leo's daughter motioned to her husband, and he quickly went to the front.

"Let's hear it for Leo and Archibald!" John said enthusiastically as his wife led her father away.

Applause thundered down on Leo, but he could not hear a thing.

Melted

"What's wrong, Lola?" Blake was mystified by the sudden reappearance of tears in his daughter's eyes, as he had only minutes before bought her a scoop of rainbow ice-cream in a cone, which seemed to brighten her day considerably. Lola turned away and stared at the sea. Not even her twin sister Lucy could get her to reveal the reason for her melancholy mood. Blake began to ask whether there was something in the bottom of her cone but decided to abandon this line of questioning mid-sentence and stare at the sea as well.

When he and the girls arrived home, Lola ran into her room and slammed the door behind her.

"Still upset?" asked Tawnee. They'd been married for six years.

"Uh-huh." Blake plonked himself down in front of the computer screen.

"Have you done your homework, Lucy?" said Tawnee.

"Yes," said Lucy. "I did it before we went out."

Tawnee narrowed her eyes. "Oh. But have you done tomorrow night's homework?"

Lucy scrunched up her face. "No," she grumped finally. "Mrs Fields will give me tomorrow night's homework tomorrow."

Tawnee narrowed her eyes further until they were almost shut. "Go to your room," she said quickly.

As Lucy trudged off to her room, Tawnee turned to her husband. "I didn't want to tell you in front of the kids," she said.

"What?" Blake said, his eyes glued to the screen.

"Taylor rang today to say he's coming home for a few days. He's booked a flight for Saturday." Taylor was Tawnee's twin brother, who had moved overseas to become a ski instructor when he was eighteen and had not set foot in his country of birth since. "He said he didn't have anywhere to stay so I said he could sleep on our couch."

Blake turned to her. "Why didn't you want to say that in front of the kids?"

"He said not to tell them so it would be a surprise."

Blake nodded slowly, his mind apparently elsewhere.

Suddenly he sprang to his feet and made his way over to his wife. "Hey, the kids are in their rooms. How 'bout it?" He brushed his wife's long blonde hair out of her eyes while simultaneously grabbing at her scarf. Tawnee slapped his hand away and strode out of the room.

The next morning Lola was still morose. "You'll feel much

better if you talk about what's on your mind," said Tawnee just before she left for work. Ultimately, her efforts amounted to nothing, as Lola had not elaborated on her feelings by the time Blake dropped her and Lucy off at school. When he returned six hours later to pick the girls up, he hoped there would be a difference in her mood. There was not.

"How was school, Lola?" he said.

"Good," she said quietly.

"Good." Blake was momentarily distracted by the sight of a young blonde mother crossing the road with her child. "And how about you, Lucy?" he added eventually.

"Good, Daddy," Lucy said cheerfully.

Lucy jumped out of the car as soon as it came to a stop. She took off running down the path, cleared the three steps leading up to the verandah and burst through the front door. She was surprised to find her mother vacuuming the couch.

"What are you doing here?" Lucy couldn't believe it. Tawnee usually arrived home an hour and a half after the girls, as her shift at the hairdressers ended at five o'clock.

"I stayed home today," Tawnee said, continuing to vacuum. "Anyway, how are you? Did you have fun today at school?"

"Are you sick?" Lucy asked in a fearful tone.

"No, no," Tawnee said. "I just thought I'd take the day off and vacuum the couch." Lucy eyed her mother suspiciously as Blake and Lola entered the house.

"Mummy!" Lola said.

"I took the day off to vacuum the couch," Tawnee said, pre-empting the question. "Is that so crazy?"

That night Blake turned to his wife in bed. "Well, this is the last night we're going to have to ourselves. As a nuclear family, I mean."

"No," she said. Ever since Tawnee gave birth to the twins, she had rebuffed all advances from her husband. Not only this, but she had also taken to covering herself up with extra clothing to actively discourage the making of advances. Blake was of the opinion that such actions were tantamount to throwing a sheet over a priceless work of art and frequently made his feelings on the matter known. These protests, however, had so far fallen on deaf ears.

"You're twenty-six, in the prime of your physical life," he cried. "It's a crime."

Tawnee rolled over and went to sleep.

The next day she drove to the airport to pick up her twin brother. In order to keep the reason for her excursion secret, she told her daughters that she was visiting her grandparents, as she knew that there would be little chance of them wanting to accompany her.

When Tawnee entered the house with her twin brother, Blake was sitting in front of the computer screen, Lola was sitting in front of the television and Lucy was in her room finishing her homework. Blake turned around and laid eyes on his brother-in-law in the flesh for the first time. His jaw dropped. He could not believe how much he looked like

Tawnee. He had acknowledged the resemblance when he was shown photographs, but in person it was uncanny.

When Blake recovered from the shock of seeing Taylor's face, he noted that his brother-in-law was wearing a t-shirt with a plunging neckline. Try as he might, he found himself unable to shift his focus from the young man's bare chest.

"Uncle Taylor!" Lola screamed when she saw him. She ran to Taylor and threw her arms around him, and Blake's gaze was broken.

"Lucy!" Tawnee shouted. "Come and see who's here!"

Taylor laughed. "Don't bother her if she's busy." As Lola loosened her grip, Taylor looked at Blake. "Hello, brother-in-law! Nice to finally meet you in person!" Blake was intrigued by Taylor's smooth, hairless chest. "I hope you've been looking after my sister!" Taylor walked up to Blake and shook his hand. "I don't know how she can wear a scarf in this weather! It's so hot!"

"Oh, you're just used to the cold," Tawnee said.

"I guess so." Taylor laughed. Lucy emerged from her bedroom and squealed. As she threw her arms around Taylor, Blake slowly made his way to the couch. His heart was beating faster than it ever had in his life.

"That was nice. I haven't had fast food for ages," Taylor said after he had finished his dinner of burgers and fries. "Not hungry, Blake?"

Blake looked up from his uneaten burger. "I'm sorry?"

"Aren't you hungry tonight, brother-in-law?" Taylor smiled and brushed his long blond hair out of his eyes.

"Uh, no," Blake said. "I had a big lunch."

Taylor nodded.

"I wish you could teach me how to ski, Uncle Taylor," Lucy said.

Taylor laughed. "I wish I could too, Lola."

"Lucy," Lucy said.

"Lucy," Taylor corrected himself. "Sorry! Unfortunately, there's not much snow around here."

"I know," she sighed.

"But, when you're old enough, you can come and visit me in the mountains, and I can teach you then."

She smiled broadly.

"Well, you must be tired after that long trip," Tawnee said as she began to gather up the empty fast-food containers.

"I am a bit," he said.

"Well, you can go to bed anytime you like," Tawnee said, gesturing to the couch. "We'll be going to bed soon, anyway, won't we, Blake?"

Blake nodded.

"Thanks." Taylor stifled a yawn. "I might take you up on that offer."

That night Blake woke up in the middle of a bad dream. It had started off pleasantly enough, with the family on a camping trip. "That should be good enough," he said as he hammered in the last tent peg. "Are you excited, girls? Your first time camping. You know, I used to go camping with my father and my brothers all the time when I was younger."

While the girls were unsure about the experience at first, eventually they came to embrace the day. By the time the evening rolled around, they were even helping Blake tend the campfire. Tawnee, however, decided early on that she was not a fan of the experience and spent the rest of the day in the tent.

When it came time to turn in for the night, Blake entered the tent first as he wanted to make sure that Tawnee was in a proper state to take the girls. He found her lying face down topless on their sleeping bag. Silently, he made his way over and sat cross-legged beside her. As he began to run his hand down her back, she stirred. Groggily, she propped herself up and focused on her husband.

To Blake's horror, he found it was not his wife, but Taylor. Had it been Taylor the whole time? Blake thought back to the morning. He was sure Tawnee had been in the seat next to him as he drove to the campsite. But if she was, where was she now? And how did Taylor get here?

"Hello, brother-in-law," Taylor said with a smile. Blake glanced down at Taylor's bare chest and let out an anguished howl.

"What the hell's wrong with you?" Blake woke and looked into the face of his wife. As she glared at him, he grabbed her chest. "You're you!" he cried.

The following morning Blake picked himself up off the bedroom floor and headed for the gym. He felt the need to pump iron as a means of re-establishing his masculinity. After spending as much time there as he was physically able, he returned home feeling much better about himself.

"The kids are next door and Taylor's gone to see Mum and Dad," Tawnee said as Blake looked around the living room. He breathed a sigh of relief, plunked himself down in front of the television and began to play a video game.

Several minutes later, Blake heard the front door open and turned around. It was Taylor. At once, fear struck his heart. Taylor was wearing a different t-shirt with a plunging neckline in addition to a pair of short shorts. Blake stared at his chest and slowly shifted his glance to his smooth thighs. It had been a long time since he had seen thighs like that. As a matter of fact, he could pinpoint the exact day.

"Hey, Blake," Taylor said.

"Hey, Taylor," Blake murmured.

"Playing a game?"

"Yeah."

"Do you want an opponent?" Blake pictured Taylor sitting next to him twisting, turning and thrusting his chest out.

"Nah," he said eventually. "I've been playing for too long as it is." He stood up and stretched his arms. "You can play if you want, though."

Taylor nodded. Blake thought he detected a slight sadness in his brother-in-law's eyes. "Well … I'm off to get some fresh air," he said quickly and before Taylor could reply, Blake was out the door.

"He thinks you're avoiding him," Tawnee told him the following day.

Blake shrugged. "Well, I haven't been," he said feebly.

Tawnee shook her head. "I think it would be nice if you went out somewhere together. Just the two of you."

Blake was thinking as he nodded.

That afternoon he took Taylor to the gym. "Do you want to do some cardio first?" Blake suggested.

Taylor nodded. He had not been to a gym before and was happy to let Blake make all the decisions. Over the next hour the two men made use of almost every piece of equipment, and Taylor managed to hold his own with Blake.

Finally, they came to the barbells. "Do you want to lift some weights?" Blake said.

"I might take a bit of a break first." Taylor took a sip from his water bottle, exhaled and stretched out on the floor. Blake nonchalantly glanced down at his brother-in-law and caught a birds-eye view of his glistening chest. Even from this height, he could make out the individual beads of perspiration. A wave of weakness suddenly came over Blake, leading him to drop the barbell he was preparing to work out with directly onto Taylor's hands.

"Can I have some more, please," Taylor said to his sister as he sat at the table with his heavily bandaged hands in his lap. Tawnee dutifully placed a spoonful of fried rice in his open mouth. Blake stared at the computer screen, attempting to tune out what was going on at the table.

"So you just ski right down?" Lucy asked her uncle.

Taylor nodded, chewing. "Yes," he said at last after swallowing. "And after you ski right down, you get on the chairlift, go back up to the top of the mountain and do it all over again."

By the time dinner had finished Taylor was weary, having answered a slew of skiing-related questions from his niece. Tawnee noticed and told the girls that it was time for bed. "And you, too," she said, shooting a glance at her husband. Blake got up from the computer and ambled off to their bedroom, secretly glad of any excuse to get away from Taylor.

The next few days Blake and Taylor avoided one another as best they could. Blake not wishing to be confronted with confusing desires and Taylor fearful that Blake might cause him further physical harm. This made the atmosphere uncomfortable. In addition, Lola's mental state appeared to be getting worse.

"It's not because I dropped the barbell on Taylor, is it?" Blake asked her one day on their way home from school. Lola shook her head, but would not elaborate.

Mercifully for Blake and Taylor, the day of Taylor's departure finally arrived.

"You two have to make up," Tawnee said to the two men at the breakfast table. "I'm not having my brother leave without being on speaking terms with my husband." She stood up and called for her daughters. When they arrived, she led them out the front door without a word.

It was Taylor who initiated the conversation. Things started off awkward, but eventually the two men came to an understanding. Blake found that if he looked at the ceiling while talking to Taylor, he could endure the conversation. An advantage was that Taylor's fear of Blake was replaced by pity, as he came to believe that Blake was not at full mental capacity.

Things got even better for Blake when he arrived at school and was greeted by *two* smiling girls. Lola would still not reveal what had caused her low mood in the first place, let alone what had happened to restore her normal disposition, but she reassured her father that she was now happier than she had ever been.

"Let's all go to the pier for ice-cream," Blake said happily when they got back home. "I'm paying."

"What ice-cream flavour would everybody like?" Blake asked when he arrived at the pier with his children and brother-in-law.

"Strawberry," Lola said.

"Chocolate," said Lucy.

"And how about you, Taylor?" Blake angled his head slightly.

Taylor looked down at his hands.

"You can hold Uncle Taylor's ice-cream, Daddy," Lola said helpfully.

Blake nodded. "Great idea, Lola. So, what's it going to be, Taylor?"

"I'll take a vanilla, if that's okay, Blake," he said.

Blake nodded. "Okay. So, one strawberry, one chocolate and one vanilla."

Taylor watched Blake walk up to the kiosk. When Blake returned, he handed one ice-cream to each of the girls and stood awkwardly near Taylor.

"I'll have a lick if it's all right, Blake," Taylor said after they had walked some distance along the pier. "Just a bit closer," he added as Blake held the ice-cream out at arm's length.

Blake realised he would have to look at Taylor to see where he was directing the ice-cream. Acting against his impulse to take off and run, Blake turned to his brother-in-law. Immediately his eyes were drawn to that plunging neckline. He proceeded to lose all feeling in his hands and drop the ice-cream scoop right into Taylor's cleavage. Taylor shrieked at the sudden cold and waved his bandaged hands around in the air.

"Get it! Get it!" he shouted.

Reluctantly, Blake stepped forward, stuck his hand down Taylor's front and attempted to fish out the icy lump. As Taylor jerked and squirmed, Blake struggled to get a hold on the scoop of vanilla ice-cream and ended up smearing it into Taylor's skin. As Blake continued to draw his hand back and forth across Taylor's chest, he began to sob.

"What's wrong, Daddy?" Lucy asked fearfully. Tears began to snake their way down Blake's cheeks and fall down Taylor's front and mix with the melted ice-cream. "Daddy? Daddy?"

The Gathering

The salt crunched under the feet of the elderly gentleman as he made his way slowly toward the centre of the plain. The sound reminded him of the time he walked across the same salt plain the previous year. The only difference between the two occasions (other than the fact that they took place one year apart) was that today the gentleman had arrived at midday while on the previous occasion he had arrived shortly before sundown. He made the decision this year to arrive early as he was eager to mingle with his fellow men for an extended period of time, an opportunity he was not afforded the previous year as the men had commenced their customary chant shortly after his arrival.

After a lengthy walk, the gentleman finally reached the centre of the salt plain. If one were to ask him how he knew he had reached the centre, he would not be able to say. All he knew was that he was there. He exhaled softly and looked around him. Salt as far as the eye could see.

He looked up. The blazing orb known as the sun was doing its best to cook his naked body. As much as it blazed, however, it stood no chance. Nothing in the world could penetrate that exterior.

The elderly gentleman continued to stand in the middle of the gleaming white disc. After several minutes, he detected movement on the horizon. Instinctively, he knew it was one of his fellow men. As the figure loomed larger, he saw the naked gentleman shared his shuffling gait and determination to reach the centre. He differed in the fact, however, that he sported a long flowing white beard which swung from side to side like a pendulum.

"Hello."

"Hello."

"Have you been here long?"

"Not long."

The first gentleman gazed at the newcomer's beard. "Looks like we're the first to arrive."

"Looks like it."

The two men stood silently for several minutes.

"This is a large salt plain," the first gentleman offered eventually.

The second gentleman grunted in agreement. "It takes a long time to reach the centre."

"I know. I hope salt is good for gout."

The second gentleman turned away and stared at the sun. "My beard drags along the ground and collects the stuff."

Upon this proclamation he slapped his beard, sending a shower of salt onto the plain.

Shortly after, another man appeared on the horizon. By the time he reached the first two, five more men had appeared.

"Hello."

"Hello. Been here long?"

"A while." The newcomer nodded and stared into space.

"The horizon is looking pretty horizontal today," the first gentleman said eventually.

The recent arrival murmured in agreement. "As of now. It can change quickly though. Yesterday morning it was looking vertical, and by the time I got out of bed it was horizontal again."

There were seventy naked men gathered in the middle of the salt plain by the time the last speck of sun sank below the horizon. The moment that happened, the men joined hands and moved outwards until they formed a large circle. It was then that they commenced their chant. The sound they produced was guttural in tone and did not resemble any language that was spoken on earth.

The chanting continued until the salt plain was swathed in darkness. When it became clear that what the men were hoping was going to happen was not going to happen, they fell silent. Slowly they unclasped hands and, upon bidding their goodbyes, began to shuffle back whence they came.

Tendril

Sitting in the snow,
A tendril,
Twined around my tongue.

Mansfield Pond

Monday

It had been a forty-minute walk from the birthplace of William Shaw to Mansfield Pond, but the spirits of the tour group members were still high.

"As you can see, this is Mansfield Pond," the tour guide announced as the tourists gazed on the famous body of water. "This pond was particularly significant in the life and career of William Shaw." Several members of the group suddenly switched their gaze from the guide to a badelynge of ducks that were waddling toward them with apparent purpose. One couple exchanged glances as the ducks increased their speed.

The tour guide gestured to a rustic bench by the pond. "While seated at this very bench, William Shaw wrote his celebrated —" He was unable to finish his sentence as he was besieged by the ducks. "Paean – to the seasons – 'Regeneration'," he said between mouthfuls of feathers. He dug the toes of his shoes into the ground in an attempt to stay upright but was ultimately brought down by the sheer weight of birds. "In order to lend his poem a realism it may not have possessed otherwise," the tour guide continued from the grass, "Shaw worked on each 'season' of the poem during each corresponding season."

By this time, the ducks had shredded the tour guide's pants and begun to peck at his bare legs. "I'm certain you would all agree with me that the result was highly effective." At that moment, the ducks appeared to decide as a group that their work was done and began to head for the pond. The tour guide struggled to his feet. "Any questions?" There was silence among the group. After giving his leg a final peck, the last remaining duck departed and joined its friends in the pond.

The tour guide stood before the group in tattered clothes. "Okay, then. Now follow me if you please, and we shall visit William Shaw's favourite watering hole."

Tuesday

"As you can see, this is Mansfield Pond," the tour guide announced. The members of the tour group stared at the body of water that lay before them. "This pond was particularly significant in the life and career of William Shaw."

"Ooh, look honey," said a woman with curly blonde hair to her husband as she pointed out a rapidly approaching badelynge of ducks. "Duckies!"

The tour guide ignored the distraction and gestured to a rustic bench by the pond. "While seated at this very bench,

William Shaw wrote his celebrated paean to the seasons 'Regeneration'." He braced himself but was ultimately bowled over by the ducks. "In order to lend his poem a realism it may not have possessed otherwise, Shaw worked on each 'season' of the poem during each corresponding season," the tour guide managed to recite despite the fact that he was face-down in the grass.

"I'm certain you would all agree with me that the result was highly effective," he continued as the ducks attacked his legs. The curly-haired woman eagerly took several photographs. Eventually, the ducks decided they had had enough and began to head for the pond. The tour guide slowly got to his feet. "Any questions?" There were none forthcoming. After giving his leg a final peck, the last remaining duck departed and joined its friends in the pond.

The tour guide stood before the group in tattered clothes. "Okay, then. Now follow me if you please, and we shall visit William Shaw's favourite watering hole."

Wednesday

After a one-and-a-half hour walk from the birthplace of William Shaw to Mansfield Pond, several of the mostly elderly members of the tour group sat down on the bench on which William Shaw had written his poem 'Regeneration' while the rest wearily sank onto the grass.

"Why don't they have more seats here?" the youngest member of the group asked the tour guide.

"As you can see, this is Mansfield Pond," the tour guide declared, ignoring the question as it was not asked during official question time. "This pond was particularly significant in the life and career of William Shaw." Because most of the group members were exhausted, they did not notice the badelynge of ducks that were coming toward them with increasing speed.

The tour guide gestured to the rustic bench by the pond that was currently occupied by several members of the tour group.

"While seated at this very bench, William Shaw wrote —" The tour guide did not get the chance to finish his sentence as he was sent flying by the badelynge of ducks. "His celebrated —" he said before spitting out a feather. "Paean to the seasons, 'Regeneration'. In order to lend his poem a realism it may not have possessed otherwise, Shaw worked on each 'season' of the poem during each corresponding season."

The ducks tore viciously at the tour guide's pants and began to peck his legs savagely. The elderly tour group members looked on blankly.

"I'm certain you would all agree with me that the result was highly effective." After most of the ducks had moved on, the tour guide gingerly got to his feet. "Any questions?" This request was met with vacant stares. After giving his leg a final peck, the last duck departed and joined its friends in the pond.

The tour guide stood before the group in tattered clothes. "Okay, then. Now follow me, if you please, and we shall visit William Shaw's favourite watering hole."

Thursday

Upon completing the thirty-minute walk from the birthplace of William Shaw to Mansfield Pond, the tour guide prepared to make his address. The fact that nobody was present was irrelevant, as he was contractually obliged to conduct the tour regardless.

"As you can see, this is Mansfield Pond," the tour guide said into the ether. "This pond was particularly significant in the life and career of William Shaw." A badelynge of ducks noticed him and came waddling.

The tour guide gestured to a rustic bench by the pond. "While seated at this very bench, William Shaw wrote his celebrated paean to the seasons 'Regene —" The tour guide was promptly bowled over by the mass of ducks. "— ration'," he continued. "In order to lend his poem a realism it may not have possessed otherwise, Shaw worked on each 'season' of the poem during each corresponding season."

"I'm certain you would all agree with me that the result was highly effective," the tour guide said as the ducks attacked his legs in a frenzy. This continued until the ducks appeared satisfied and departed. The tour guide struggled to his feet and asked if anyone had any questions. There was no response.

After giving his leg a final peck, the last duck departed and joined its friends in the pond.

The tour guide stood before what would have been the group if there had been one in tattered clothes. "Okay, then. Now follow me if you please, and we shall visit William Shaw's favourite watering hole."

Friday

"Is this Mansfield Pond?" A balding man in a royal blue polo shirt asked the tour guide.

"As you can see, this is Mansfield Pond," the tour guide announced, ignoring the question from the gentleman, one of two people who made up the day's tour group. "This pond was particularly significant in the life and career of William Shaw."

"Hello! What's happening here?" said the other member of the party, a bug-eyed individual in a Hawaiian shirt. He had just spotted a badelynge of ducks making their way toward the small party at breakneck speed.

"Is that the bench William Shaw sat on when he wrote 'Regeneration'?" the man in the royal blue polo shirt asked as the tour guide gestured to a rustic bench by the pond.

"While seated at this very bench, William Shaw wrote his celebrated paean to the seasons, 'Regeneration'. In order to lend his poem a realism —" A duck made contact with the face of the tour guide, causing him to stop mid-sentence.

"It may not have possessed otherwise," the tour guide finished. He opened his mouth in order to begin his next sentence but was brought down by a flurry of birds. "Shaw worked on each 'season' of the poem during each corresponding season," the tour guide said as he lay sprawled on the grass.

"Would you like some help there?" asked the man in the Hawaiian shirt, as the ducks began to peck the tour guide's legs.

"I'm certain you would all agree with me that the result was highly effective," the tour guide continued. As the man in the Hawaiian shirt began to make his way over to the tour guide the ducks decided they had had enough and turned around and headed for the pond. The two members of the tour group proceeded to help the tour guide to his feet. "Any questions?" the tour guide asked.

"Are you all right?" said the man in the royal blue polo shirt. The tour guide nodded. After giving his leg a final peck, the last remaining duck departed and joined its friends in the pond.

The tour guide stood in tattered clothes before the two men. "Okay, then. Now follow me, if you please, and we shall visit William Shaw's favourite watering hole."

Findings Regarding the Motives
Behind the Installation of Eight Signs
in the Greater Greenvale Area

Upon coming across a sign, it must be said that most of us would obey its instruction. Very few of us, however, would stop to consider who had installed the sign and why. Is this not a most important question? In not considering this question, we are putting our trust fully in an anonymous individual. We could be blindly obeying a sign that has been erected by an individual with mischief on their mind or, worse still, malice. As a means of alerting the general public to this matter, I decided to make note of every sign I came across over a twenty-four-hour period, discover who erected it and why, and publish my findings in the local newspaper.

While the investigation was on the whole successful and the findings were what I considered of interest to the general public, the editor of the local newspaper was unwilling to publish the results. Following this rejection, I presented my findings to the local magazine. Alas, the editor of the local magazine also declined to publish my study. After receiving rejections from close to one hundred local, national and international publications, including Sign Enthusiasts Monthly, I made the decision to self-publish my findings. Here they are:

Sign No. 1: Stop Sign
(At the Intersection of Main and Third Street)

I came across this sign while I was driving my automobile. After stopping and giving way to the traffic coming down Third Street, I made my way to my local council building, as I had read that the council were responsible for installing road signs. I parked out the front and went inside. A receptionist flashed me a broad smile when I approached. After we exchanged pleasantries, I told her I wanted to see the holder of the Transport portfolio, Councillor Purcell. She told me I would not be able to see him immediately, as he was in a meeting, but if I so desired, I could wait until the meeting concluded and see him then if he was not too busy. When I replied that that would be wonderful, she pointed to a row of chairs that dotted the front of the room on either side of the door and suggested I take a seat.

After fourteen minutes of waiting, a door to the left opened and a steady stream of councillors flowed out. I got up quickly, made my way over to Councillor Purcell and grabbed his arm tightly. I then asked him who had installed the stop sign at the intersection of Main Street and Third Street. "Well, we don't keep a record of which individual installs which sign, but I can tell you it would have been a council worker," he said. I then asked him why the sign was installed, and he replied that it was so vehicles did not crash into each other at the intersection of Main Street and Third Street. I was satisfied with his response, so I thanked him for his time, loosened my grip on his arm and departed.

Sign No. 2: Speed Limit Sign
(On Main Street Between Third and Fourth Street)

I returned to the site of the stop sign on Main Street and Third Street, then continued along. Soon I came to a sign displaying the speed limit. I knew at once I would need to return to the council building and speak with Councillor Purcell in order to find out who installed the sign and why. Driving at a speed which was comfortably below the limit, I arrived back at the council building and parked my automobile out the front. When I walked in, I saw Councillor Purcell in conversation with a woman I presumed to be a fellow councillor. He turned his head and looked at me as I approached and he raised his eyebrows.

"Hello," he said as he put his arms behind his back. "Do you want to see me?" I nodded. "Why don't you take a seat and I'll be over in a minute." I nodded and went and sat down in the chair I had occupied before.

After six minutes, Councillor Purcell came over and asked me if he could do anything for me. I told him I wanted to know who installed the speed limit sign on Main Street just beyond Third Street and why.

"Well," he replied slowly, "as I said before, we don't keep a record of which individual installs which sign, but you can rest assured it was a council worker. And, in answer to your second question, the sign would have been installed in order to remind drivers to stay at or below the speed limit in order to reduce accidents on the road." I nodded and thanked him for his help. He smiled slightly and I departed again.

Sign No. 3: Stop Sign
(At the Intersection of Main and Fourth Street)

After returning to the speed limit sign on Main Street, I continued along and eventually came to another stop sign. This one was at the intersection of Main Street and Fourth Street. I knew what I had to do. After parking my automobile out the front of the council building, I walked inside and looked around for Councillor Purcell.

"Are you looking for Councillor Purcell?" the receptionist asked. I nodded. "I'm afraid he left several minutes ago," she said. "I can take a message if you like." As I began to relay my two questions, I noticed several automobiles through a window to the right. I wondered to myself if this was the council members' private car park.

"Is that the council members' private car park?" I asked the receptionist.

"Yes —" she began to answer, and I made for the door. "He's gone, sir," she called, but I threw open the door and ran around to the side of the building.

As I approached the car park, I saw Councillor Purcell about to get into his automobile. When he saw me he went pale.

"Hello, councillor," I called. "I have a couple of questions for you."

"I'm sorry," he said. "I have to go."

"I'll be quick."

He sighed and looked up at the clouds. "Okay. Ask away."

"I was wondering who erected the stop sign at the intersection of Main Street and Fourth Street and why."

He stared at me a long while and sighed again. "As I've told you twice already, we don't have information on which individual has installed which sign. And my answer to your second question is the same as my answer to your earlier question: it was installed to stop vehicles crashing into each other at the intersection. There. Are you satisfied?"

I nodded.

"Good. Now can I ask *you* a question?"

I nodded.

"Can you promise me you won't bother me in the future with any further questions regarding road signs?"

I nodded.

"Thank you," he said as he got into his automobile.

Sign No. 4: Lollipop Sign
(On Main Street Between Fourth and Fifth Street)

I sat in my automobile at the intersection of Main Street and Fourth Street watching the thinning traffic and felt great satisfaction with the way my investigation was going. Councillor Purcell had seemed happy to answer my questions, and he had provided detailed answers. I wondered what would happen, however, when I came across a sign that was not installed by a council worker.

Eventually my path cleared, and I was able to continue on my way. After seventeen seconds I came to a school crossing. I watched as a stream of children began to make their way across, guarded by a lollipop lady with a lollipop sign in her hand. After I had slowed to a stop, I quickly wound down my window.

"Hello, lollipop lady," I called after I had stuck my head out. She did not answer. "Hello, lollipop lady," I repeated.

She stared at me. "Are you crazy or something?"

I shook my head. "No," I said. "I just want to ask you a couple of questions."

"I'm busy making sure these children cross the road safely."

"I'll be quick," I said.

She shook her head. "You'll have to pull over."

I nodded and pulled over to the side of the road.

The lollipop lady narrowed her eyes at me as I walked up to her.

"I was wondering who installed the sign in your hand and why they did so," I said quickly.

"Are you trying to be funny?"

"No," I said. "I sincerely want to know. I'm conducting a study."

"Okay —" she said. "Nobody installed the sign in my hand. I picked it up myself. And I guess the answer to your other question is I picked it up so I could hold it and get people to stop their cars so children can cross the road safely. Is that what you wanted to know?"

I nodded. "Thank you very much," I said. "You've just contributed to a very important study."

Sign No. 5: Beware of ? Sign
(On Main Street Between Fourth and Fifth Street)

After I got into my automobile and rejoined traffic, I began to scan fences for signs. In just four seconds, I spotted one. Unfortunately, I was unable to make out the words from my automobile, so I had to pull over and take a closer look. When I was within seeing distance, I realised it said 'Beware of ?' in large black letters. I shrugged, opened the gate and entered the front yard. After making my way along a paved path edged with daisies, I came to a small porch. I was about to knock on the door when a small creature that looked like a cross between a dragon and a toupee bounded up to me from nowhere and sank its razor-sharp teeth into my right leg. I shrieked and began to bang on the door with both fists.

An elderly woman eventually opened it and laughed in my face.

"Didn't you read the sign?" she said, her bare gums glistening. She looked at the creature. "Come on, love. That's enough." She pushed it off me with a straw broom and beckoned me inside. "Come in. I'll bandage your leg."

Gasping, I sat down at her kitchen table and allowed her to bandage my leg. When she had finished, I broached the subject of her sign.

"Did you put up that sign?" I asked, trying to ignore the pain in my leg.

"No, my son put it up," she said. "He insisted upon it!" She laughed.

"I see," I said. The woman had inadvertently answered my second question. "I suppose I'd better get going." I got shakily to my feet. I wanted to get away from this woman and her pet as soon as possible. She grinned and returned the roll of bandages to what I took to be its customary place on the table just inside the front door. "Take care!" she said as I stepped outside. As I made my way down the steps of her porch onto the paved path edged with daisies, the creature jumped out from behind a rosebush and sank its teeth into my left leg.

Sign No. 6: Speed Limit Sign
(On Main Street Between Fourth and Fifth Street)

When the elderly woman had finished bandaging my left leg, she escorted me off her premises, making sure to keep the creature away from me with her straw broom. I could hear her cackle even after I'd pulled the door of my automobile shut. I started the engine and pulled onto the road. I tried to focus on the road as a means of distracting me from the searing pain in both of my legs. It did not work.

I soon came to another speed limit sign. As I gazed at the number in the centre of the circle, I realised there was only one man who could tell me who had installed the sign and why. After I pulled over to the side of the road, I reached into my pocket and took out my cellular phone. After fifty-seven seconds of searching, I found the phone number of Councillor Purcell. I dialled it and waited for him to answer. After several rings, Councillor Purcell's voice came on the line.

"Hello?"

"Hello," I said. "Is this Councillor Purcell?"

"Yes."

"Ah, that's wonderful. I was wondering if I could ask you a couple of questions."

There was a silence of eight seconds. "Hello? Are you still there, Councillor Purcell?"

"You. I thought I asked you not to contact me with any more questions."

"I know you said that, Councillor Purcell. But these questions are very important. I just wanted to know who installed the speed limit sign on Main Street between Fourth and Fifth Street."

The line went dead.

I immediately dialled Councillor Purcell's number again. "Hello," he said.

"Hello, Councillor Purcell," I said. "I think we got cut off."

The line went dead again. We were not having any luck at all. I dialled the number again, but this time he was even unable to answer. I sat in my automobile and pondered what I should do next.

I pulled into Councillor Purcell's driveway and looked up at his house. It was quite grand, with its roof and windows. I thought to myself how lucky it was that I was able to find the councillor's address on my phone. I got out of my automobile gingerly and hobbled to the front door, which sported a golden knocker. Eagerly, I grasped it and knocked several times. A woman who I took to be Councillor Purcell's wife opened the door and squinted at me.

"Hello," I said. "Is this the home of Councillor Purcell?"

"Yes."

"I've got a couple of questions for him," I said. "I was about to ask them on the phone, but we got cut off. Can I see him?"

The woman stared at me. "I'll tell him you're here and if he's not too busy he might see you," she said eventually. "Just wait there."

It was thirty-one minutes later that a police car pulled into the driveway and came to a stop behind my automobile. Two police officers got out and walked up to me.

"Hello, officers," I said with a smile. "Come to arrest Councillor Purcell for making me wait so long to see him?"

Neither answered me. One grabbed my arms roughly, pulled them behind my back and handcuffed me.

"Have I done something wrong?" I said.

"You were warned to stop harassing Councillor Purcell and you didn't heed the warning," said the one who didn't handcuff me.

"So you're taking a trip with us to the station."

Sign No. 7: 'Police' Sign
(Out the Front of Police Station)

The two officers pulled me out of the police car and began to lead me to the station when I spotted a large sign that read 'Police'. I was overcome with joy.

"Excuse me, officers," I said excitedly. "Who put up that big sign there?"

There was no answer, so I asked my second question: "Why was that sign put up?"

There was no answer to that question either.

Sign No. 8: 'Holding Cell' Sign
(Inside Police Station)

After I had gone through the process of providing fingerprints and so on, I was led to a holding cell by another officer. I knew it was a holding cell, as there was a small sign on the door that said so.

"Officer, who put that sign there?" I asked.

Unfortunately, I was pushed into the cell and had the door closed behind me before I had a chance to hear the officer's reply.

Vacant

If One Should Encounter
the Fliffle

One of the most uplifting experiences one can have on the planet known as Earth is meeting the being known as the Fliffle. Whether one is undergoing a crisis or is just feeling low at the point one encounters the Fliffle, one is sure to feel fully pepped after the meeting. For the unlucky few that have not yet encountered the Fliffle, the following is a compendium of facts regarding the being so one will know what to expect should an encounter occur.

The Fliffle often appears in the most unlikely of places, such as inside buildings that are in the process of being demolished, atop trees that are in the process of being felled and in books that are in the process of being written. Concurrent with said appearance, a sound will be heard, to the highly tuned ear a 'blip' and to the lowly tuned ear nothing at all. One will know one is in the presence of the Fliffle as its body will be enrobed in a tunic of the finest brocade, its head will be topped with a cream pillbox hat and its fingers will be adorned with white gold jewellery.

The type of greeting used by the Fliffle is dependent on environment. If, for example, one encounters the Fliffle at the bottom of the ocean, it will almost certainly remark upon the dampness of the surroundings. If one encounters the Fliffle in a garden, it will no doubt comment on the scent of the flowers. Wherever one encounters the Fliffle, one is sure to be greeted in a friendly fashion.

When the proverbial ice is broken, the Fliffle will attempt to discern whether its counsel is required. This is done by performing a graceful dance then blowing into a rudimentary musical instrument resembling a flute. If the audience has not departed by the time the piercing note has faded, the Fliffle will take this as evidence that its presence is desired.

The Fliffle will then proceed to dispense several nuggets of wisdom with disconcerting rapidity. After this attempt to enrich the individual's life, the Fliffle will stomp the ground several times and whinny like a horse. With this, the encounter is over, and the Fliffle will depart in order to find another downhearted soul.

Your Lucky Day

"Hi! These seats are quite small, aren't they? You're lucky you have a window seat so you can pretend you're not on a train at all. I have no choice but to accept the reality that I'm on a train. Unless I close my eyes, of course. Then I can imagine I'm anywhere I want to be. I can close my eyes and be on the summit of a mountain. Ooh, it's cold! Brr! You don't have any extra clothes, do you? A spare jacket or two? No, that's all right. I'm only role-playing.

"I love autumn. The colours of the leaves on the trees are so pretty. I remember when I was a child my grandmother used to have a garden full of trees and I used to spend hours playing in the fallen leaves. I used to spend hours in that garden. Discovering all the different life forms. So fun. Did you used to do that when you were a child? Run around looking for bugs and things? Oh. I did. That's when I became aware of the life force. The life force. The life force that is present in all creatures.

"I remember the first time I realised that each creature has a life force. I was watching a ladybird walk across a leaf. Then it hit me. This ladybird is emitting its energy into the atmosphere. It is literally secreting its energy into the atmosphere. Isn't that wonderful? To have such a realisation at such a young age. From then on, I've communicated with every creature I've come across. I tune into their life force and they tune into mine naturally.

"That's another thing. All animals tune into our life force naturally. We have to learn how to tune into theirs, but they tune into ours naturally. How did I? It just became obvious when I stepped onto the ladybird's plane. It will become apparent to you when you open yourself up to the secretion. Of course. Every living creature secretes this energy. When you fully understand this, you know that we are all truly one. That day, that ladybird entered my body, and I entered the body of the ladybird. All without touching! It walked around in my skin and I in turn possessed it and experienced flight. Absolutely. I've been inside you and you've been inside me since the beginning of time. This is your station? Oh. Hey, it was lovely talking to you. Bye!"

Is the Human Being a Farmer,
a Harvester or a Seed?

Is the human being a farmer, a harvester or a seed? Such a question can only be answered after extensive deliberation. Multiple factors must be considered, for example, whether one possesses the gift of autonomy, whether one is subservient to another and whether one has the ability to sprout and take on another form.

Picture a farmer. There he is, sitting in his favourite chair in the farmhouse he built when he was a much younger man. He is asleep presently, but imagine all the crops he must have planted throughout his life. Whatever number you thought of, the actual number is probably much higher. With his gnarled, brown hands this salt-of-the-earth character scattered the seeds that grew to become the wheat that was used to make the bread for the people of his town. Or perhaps the seeds became pumpkins, which were used by the deputy mayor's wife to make her famous pumpkin pies. Perhaps the seeds grew to become watermelons that were thrown by the deputy mayor's wife at the deputy mayor after he mistakenly dug up her prized petunias. And still the farmer sleeps.

He has many pictures hanging on the walls of his farmhouse, more than likely hung by himself when his hands were less gnarled and brown, or possibly when they were gnarled and white, or brown and not yet gnarled. Or maybe somebody else hung them. One picture in the middle of the wall facing the farmer appears to depict the farmer and his significant other, from a time long ago judging by the clothes the pair are wearing and the hairstyle of the significant other. She does not appear to live in the farmhouse, she may have passed on or left the farmer to be with another. Perhaps it was a mutual separation.

The picture to the right of the farmer and his potential significant other appears to depict the farmer and his two brothers. They all have the same upturned nose and prominent chin. The picture to the left could be of a distant relative, considering the lack of facial similarity. Perhaps it is a great-aunt. At last, the farmer stirs in his chair. He opens his eyes slowly and stares into space for several seconds. He rises from his chair. He walks briskly to the window and gazes at his field. It is not resplendent with wheat, pumpkins or watermelons, as it is not harvesting season. Perhaps let us imagine a different farmer, a young farmer, married with two children, gazing out of his window at the beginning of harvesting season. This farmer grows cabbages, and his eyes are fixated on them. The leafy delights are ripe for the plucking.

This is where one can begin to consider the question at hand. Is the human being a farmer? Well, this human being certainly is, judging by his hat. But is the human being in general a farmer? This question is more difficult to answer. If one considers the farmer a metaphor for one who is in control of one's life and sows one's crop in order to harvest the results, then it may be concluded that a human being is a farmer. However, if one does not put one's ideas into practice, does one have the right to call oneself a farmer? The answer must be no.

The question must also be asked if one is producing a crop for business or pleasure. If the answer is the latter, this may disqualify the individual from being a farmer. If the answer is the former, one must consider the grey area of whether the intended production of a crop for commercial purposes qualifies one as a farmer or if a crop has to be produced in order for one to assume the title. If one plants a crop in good faith but is unfortunate to have one's crop fail, can one call oneself a farmer? If the definition pertains to the intention, then by all means, one has every right to call oneself a farmer. However, if the definition pertains to the production of a crop, then one would not be able to call oneself a farmer.

Let us return to the farmer. As he surveys his crop, he ponders whether now is the appropriate time to harvest said crop, using the new harvester he bought in preparation for harvesting season. He decides that yes, now *is* the time, and so he begins to make his way to his shed, where he keeps his harvester. As he walks, he takes in his surroundings: the green grass, the wide-open spaces, the country air. There is no place he would rather be. Eventually, he comes to his shed. He slides the door open. There it is. His brand-new harvester. As he puts the key in the ignition, his grin grows to the point where it could not possibly grow wider.

This brings us back to our original question. Is the human being a harvester? While it has been surmised that the farmer is in complete control of his actions, the same cannot be said of the harvester. While the harvester is able to move of its own accord in the instance that the farmer falls off, in most cases the farmer wields control. Therefore, in order for the human being to be a harvester, they would be subservient to another person except in the event of an escape. This situation bears some similarity with a hostage situation, save for one very important difference. The issue of autonomy. While the farmer is always in full control of his actions, the harvester does not possess the trait of autonomy which is present in most humans and animals. This is why the harvester cannot stop when the farmer yells at it to do so.

It can also be said that the harvester exhibits the behaviour of an individual who has been hypnotised or is under some other kind of mind control. Being hypnotised will rob an individual of their autonomy, although it must be said that hypnosis is not normally a permanent state, unless the hypnotist is particularly sinister. Therefore, it must be concluded that while the human being does bear some similarities to the harvester, namely a lack of autonomy when one is under hypnosis or other variation of mind control, ultimately it is not a harvester.

After the farmer harvests his cabbages, he packs them into crates in preparation for his trip to the market on Sunday. All the cabbages that is, except one. He holds this particular cabbage in his hands and breathes in the aroma. It is the aroma of autonomy. The farmer stands fixed to the spot, unable to take his eyes off the fruit of his labours. Holding it gently as if it were a sacred jewel, the farmer slowly brings the cabbage to his face, lips trembling. Then, as if there were a chance the cabbage could disappear, the farmer thrusts it against his mouth, lips parted and teeth bared, and proceeds to burrow his way to the other side in the manner an incensed hare would go through a ball of soft cheese. Suddenly, all the farmer is left with is a wet ring of cabbage spinning around his neck like a hula hoop. Autonomy. He relished it!

After the farmer returned to reality, he returned to his farmhouse to prepare for planting season. What would he plant this season? Pineapples? Custard apples? Papayas? When it came time for planting, the farmer planted what he hoped would be the finest crop of cabbages that would ever come to harvest.

Finally, let us consider whether a human being is a seed. Not in a literal sense of course, but in a metaphorical sense.

While the farmer has complete control over his actions and the harvester can carry out actions but has no control over them, the seed can do neither. It simply exists to grow into a plant and bear either fruits or vegetables. One similarity that *does* exist between the seed and the harvester is that neither possesses the farmer's gift of autonomy, which means that the human being is not a seed.

And so, after promised deliberation, it has come time to decide whether the human being is a farmer, a harvester or a seed. As one watches the farmer wander around among his veritable bounty of cabbages (harvesting season comes along so quickly), one might come to the conclusion that the question itself is irrelevant, and simply inhale the country air.

Mass Sty Repurposing

Two things have happened since the pigs were set free. One, the streets have become overrun with pigs. Two, the sties formerly occupied by the pigs have been reclassified as 'disused'.

While the former may appear a significant inconvenience, it is important to note that the only individuals affected by this occurrence were those that were walking the streets and those that were planning on walking the streets. The latter could be said to be detrimental to a greater percentage of the population, as the sight of a disused sty has been found to produce feelings of distress in the beholder, according to several peer-reviewed studies.

Following are three examples of pig farmers repurposing their sties in the wake of the mass release, in an attempt to lessen feelings of distress among members of the general public.

The first pig farmer (Arthur) decided to become a watermelon farmer as a result of the decree and is now onto his third crop planted on the site of his former sty. Every morning he stands and gazes at his melons the way he once gazed at his pigs. If it is particularly early in the morning and he has not yet fully woken, he will occasionally believe he is still a pig farmer and begin to worry that none of his pigs are moving. It is only when he ventures closer and discovers that the pigs are cool and smooth to the touch as opposed to warm and furry that he remembers his current occupation and his blood pressure returns to normal.

The second pig farmer (Arthur) decided to donate his sty to the local agricultural museum so it could be preserved for the benefit of future generations. The excavation was a sizeable task, but once the sty was installed in the main hall of the museum, it was agreed by all involved that the result was well worth the time and effort. As a matter of fact, Arthur himself declared at the unveiling that he had never seen the sty look better.

Lastly, the third pig farmer (Arthur) decided to transform his sty into a dance studio so the local dance students would have a venue in which to practise their routines. The facility was well-received by the general public, with the walls and roof drawing a sizeable amount of praise. It was only the absence of a floor that attracted a negative response. Regrettably, this issue could not be rectified as Arthur had spent the money that could have gone to a floor on a diamond-studded hat. Nevertheless, the students made the best of a bad situation, and put on an end-of-year performance at the local theatre in their mud-caked outfits for the members of the public who were able to make it in without being trampled by pigs.

133

Deep Fried

Mark stood over the deep fryer and gazed into the bubbling oil. "I hope the chip never decides to rise up against the cook," he thought to himself. "Because if it does —"

"Two dollars' worth of chips and a burger with the lot, please," he heard a customer say behind his back.

"Two dollars' worth of chips and a burger with the lot, please," parroted his wife.

It was a busy night at Mark and Tilly's food truck, but Mark was okay with busy nights. After two decades in business, he was confident he could handle anything that came his way. He was across the ingredients, the cooking equipment and the money he received which made the five hours working in this aluminium sauna worthwhile. The only variable he could not entirely control were the customers, though he found in most cases they differed only slightly. They were usually peckish, exhibited a restless demeanour and possessed a face one would not expect to see in a high-class restaurant. There were of course exceptions, such as the distinguished gentleman who appeared later that night and would come to dominate Mark's thoughts over the next three weeks.

For approximately the fiftieth time that night Mark glanced at his watch. Nine-thirty. Half an hour until closing time. As Mark and his wife swapped places, a portly gentleman waddled up to the serving window and requested half a dozen doughnuts. After Mark relayed the order to his wife, the gentleman stepped back to wait while a young woman with a ponytail took his place and requested two pieces of fish and three dollars' worth of chips. By the time Mark had relayed this order, Tilly had already placed the two pieces of fish in the fryer to the right of the fryer in which the chips were cooking and to the left of the fryer in which the six doughnuts were cooking.

As Mark took the young woman's money and deposited it in the cash register, he noticed a middle-aged gentleman arrive. This man did not look like his typical customer. He was wearing an expensive-looking navy suit and a royal blue tie in addition to fashionable brown shoes. When one took into account the gentleman's attire and the fact that he exuded an educated air, it was not difficult for one to imagine that he was a member of the upper crust. After handing the woman her change, he prepared for the mysterious gentleman to come forward.

"Hello, sir," Mark said nervously, trying to appear as though it was a regular occurrence that a gentleman of this man's calibre patronised his food truck. "What would you like?"

The gentleman looked about anxiously, as if he expected to be mugged. "I'd like a —" He quickly scanned the menu above the serving window. "Burger. With the lot. Yes, a burger with the lot, thank you."

Mark nodded. "Anything else?"

The gentleman looked around again and inched closer to the window. "As a matter of fact, yes," he said in a voice just loud enough for Mark to hear. "Could you deep-fry the burger, by any chance?"

Mark's eyes widened. "I – suppose so." He turned around and whispered the man's request to Tilly, who shrugged and started work on the burger.

Suddenly, Mark remembered the other orders. Moving swiftly, he took the doughnuts out of the right fryer, dusted them with cinnamon sugar and placed them in a crisp white paper bag.

"Six doughnuts," he called to the first gentleman. The man hurried up to the window, collected his order with a smile and left. As Tilly placed the bun on top of the distinguished gentleman's burger, Mark turned to the left fryer and took out the chips. As he placed tongfuls onto the paper wrapping, he heard a voice from behind tell him to hurry up, in no uncertain terms. Mark sprinkled the salt on and wiped his brow, doing his best to ignore the comment. He rarely got flustered, but the presence of the distinguished gentleman had him rattled. He quickly wrapped up the chips and turned to the window.

"Three dollars' worth of chips," he called to the young woman.

"Are the two pieces of fish in there?" she said.

"Oh, no – sorry!" Mark darted to the middle fryer, took out the pieces of fish and dumped them onto the paper. After quickly sprinkling them with salt, he wrapped them up and handed the bundle to the woman, who scowled and left.

Mark spun around and watched his wife make her way over to the middle fryer with the burger, set it in the basket and lower it into the bubbling oil. This was an act that had not been attempted before in his humble truck and Mark was keen to see the result with his own eyes. When Tilly raised the basket, Mark gasped. What he saw before him was a deep-fried burger. Nothing more, nothing less. Tilly quickly wrapped up the burger and nodded in the direction of the gentleman. After the man collected his order and left, Mark stumbled out of the food truck and exhaled heavily.

Over the next week, Mark found it difficult to concentrate on his work. He continued to confuse orders, with Tilly often having to step in and pick up the slack. The face of the distinguished gentleman popped into his mind at the most inopportune moments, such as when he was staring into a beef patty or kissing his wife. Still, he pushed on.

On Friday night, Mark glanced at his watch and noticed it was almost nine-thirty. As his wife handed a red-headed gentleman two dollars' worth of chips and three pieces of fish, Mark spotted a dark figure making its way toward the truck. As the figure stepped out of the darkness, Mark's heart leapt into his throat. It was the distinguished gentleman. Tonight, he was wearing a black suit, a red patterned tie and what appeared to be the same brown shoes.

"Hello again," said Mark, attempting to strike a tone that was familiar enough to put the man at ease without being familiar enough to make him feel that Mark had friendship on his mind.

"Hello," the man said.

"What would you like?"

"May I have a burger —" The man looked up at the menu as he had the week before. "With the lot."

Mark nodded and was about to start making the burger when the man leant forward. "Could you deep-fry it, please?"

Mark's blood ran cold. What was this man playing at? Why would a man of such obvious high standing order a deep-fried burger with the lot not just once, but twice? He smiled weakly. "I can," he managed to murmur.

As Tilly walked past him and handed a teenage girl a bundle, Mark stumbled to the food preparation area like a zombie. Trembling, he grabbed a bun from the bag and dropped it onto the floor. After mopping his brow, he bent down and picked it up before Tilly took it from his hand and tossed it into the bin. Following this, she took over the preparation of the burger and sent Mark to the corner of the truck, where he sat down on a plastic chair and watched the proceedings.

The distinguished gentleman stood half in the shadows, not keen on being seen but not wanting to give Mark and Tilly the impression that he had left. When Tilly came to the window with the burger, he hurried up to receive his order and with a brief word of thanks hurried off just as quickly. Mark resumed service shortly after, still shaken by the episode. While they had several more customers before they closed for the day, Mark could not get the distinguished gentleman out of his mind.

Over the next week Mark described the man to several of his regular customers and asked if they knew him. No one did.

"I just don't understand it," Mark said to his wife during one of their slower periods. "He's obviously a man of taste. Look at his shoes! Why would he want a deep-fried burger with the lot?"

"What are you asking me for?" Tilly rested on the plastic chair.

Mark sighed. "It's just bugging me, that's all." By the time Friday rolled around, tomatoes, doughnuts and pineapple rings had all hit the floor as a result of Mark's skittishness.

Just after seven-thirty, one of Mark and Tilly's regular customers arrived. He was an unpredictable senior citizen with a lazy eye and a liking for hot doughnuts. Mark immediately decided to attempt to coerce him into finding out as much about the mystery gentleman as possible.

"The usual, Mack," the man said good-naturedly.

Mark nodded, then beckoned him closer. "Say, Clive, do you think you could do me a favour?"

Clive's face fell. "Well, it depends on the favour."

Mark leaned out of the window and spoke softly into the old man's ear. "Would you mind coming back in two hours? Only I —"

Clive put his hand up. "Sorry, Mack. Can't use that much petrol in a day. I'm on a pension, you know."

Mark thought to himself. "What if I gave you free dough-nuts for a month?"

He saw Clive was torn. "Well… "

"You'd be doing me a huge favour," Mark said.

"Well, okay, Mack," Clive relented. "But I wouldn't do it for anybody else." Mark waited until Tilly had served the customers who had arrived while they were talking, then filled Clive in on his plan.

As nine-thirty ticked over, Clive was nowhere to be seen. As Mark cursed the elderly man under his breath, a drawn young man arrived, followed shortly after by the distinguished gentleman. The young man ordered a burger with bacon, lettuce and tomato while the distinguished gentleman predictably ordered a deep-fried burger with the lot. Mark noticed he was wearing a purple suit with a purple-and-white striped tie and his customary brown shoes. He also thought he may have seen cufflinks, though he was not sure.

As Tilly started on their orders, Mark noticed the young

man walk over to the older man and strike up a conversation. Seeing this, Mark turned around and whispered to Tilly to slow down. By the time she finished the orders, the men were becoming restless. As Tilly started to make her way to the window, Mark snatched the bags from her and shot her a knowing look. Mark called the distinguished gentleman over and handed him the bag.

"Enjoy!" he said as the man turned and hurried away.

When he called the younger man over, he grilled him on the topic of the conversation.

"I don't know, general chit-chat," the man said. "You know, how's your day been and stuff like that."

"He didn't say what he did for a living, did he?"

"As a matter of fact, he did. He said he was a doctor."

Mark stood, open-mouthed. "Anything else?" he managed to utter.

The man shook his head. "Not that I can remember."

Over the next week Mark put together a plan to find out why the distinguished gentleman patronised his food truck. On Friday, when the man left with his order, Mark was going to slip out of the truck, leaving Tilly to run the business solo for the final half hour. He was then going to take note of which car the distinguished gentleman got into and follow him home. He would then bug the man's house in the hope that he would let slip the reason a gentleman such as he would order a deep-fried burger with the lot from a food truck every Friday night at nine-thirty.

Mark served his customers that night with one eye on his watch. He was happy for the patronage, but eager for nine-thirty to roll along. When it finally did, Mark was a bundle of nerves. He began to stress that the man would not show up that night, or worse still, that he would never show up again. He was pacing up and down the confines of the truck when the customer in question finally arrived. As the man dictated his order to Tilly, Mark began to shake, and ducked out of view of the serving window. Mark watched Tilly make the burger, lower it into the fryer and lift it up again, a sequence that seemed to last an eternity. After Tilly handed the man his burger and said goodbye, Mark quickly kissed her and slipped out of the truck into the cold night air.

From what he judged to be a safe distance, Mark watched the distinguished gentleman make his way toward his car. When he got in and shut the door, he slipped inside his own car and double-checked his equipment. When he was one hundred percent sure everything was there, he started the ignition with a shaky hand.

As Mark tailed the distinguished gentleman's car, he began to have second thoughts about his plan. He had been so focused on solving the mystery he had not thought of what would happen if he got caught. Now, in the comparative quiet of his car, the possible consequences crossed his mind for the first time. When he was on the verge of turning around, the vision of the man walking away with the deep-fried burger came into his mind and all thoughts of returning to his food truck disappeared.

After several minutes, the distinguished gentleman turned left and pulled into a petrol station. Mark slowed to a halt by the kerb and slouched down as much as he could in his seat, while keeping an eye on the man's car. "So this is what it feels like to be a private detective," Mark thought to himself. After a brief period, the man rejoined the traffic, and Mark resumed his pursuit.

Eventually, the distinguished gentleman pulled into his driveway. As a means of avoiding suspicion, Mark continued on and parked his car by the kerb several houses down. He remained in his seat until he heard a car door slam, then gathered his equipment and got out of the car. Quietly, he crept toward the man's house and hid behind trees and hedges to avoid being seen.

In the midst of an exploratory lap around the distinguished gentleman's house, Mark found himself approaching the window of a lit room. Curious, he poked his head around just far enough to see inside. It appeared to be a living room. With his hand over his mouth, Mark watched the distinguished gentleman make his way across the floor and hand the burger to a woman he took to be the gentleman's wife.